CHOCOLATE GOODIES

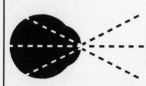

This Large Print Book carries the Seal of Approval of N.A.V.H.

CHOCOLATE GOODIES

JACQUELIN THOMAS

THORNDIKE PRESS

A part of Gale, Cengage Learning

GALE
CENGAGE Learning™

Detroit • New York • San Francisco • New Haven, Conn • Waterville, Maine • London

GALE
CENGAGE Learning™

LIBRARY OF CONGRESS CATALOGING-IN-PUBLICATION DATA

Thomas, Jacquelin.
   Chocolate goodies / by Jacquelin Thomas.
    p. cm. — (Thorndike Press large print African-American)
   ISBN-13: 978-1-4104-2412-9 (hardcover : alk. paper)
   ISBN-10: 1-4104-2412-X (hardcover : alk. paper)
   1. Confectioners—Fiction. 2. Millionaires—Fiction. 3. African Americans—Fiction. 4. Los Angeles (Calif.)—Fiction. 5. Large type books. I. Title.
PS3570.H5637C48 2010
813'.54—dc22   2010002139

Published in 2010 by arrangement with Harlequin Books S.A.

Printed in the United States of America
1 2 3 4 5 6 7 14 13 12 11 10

Dear Reader,
February is the month of love!

I love Valentine's Day and everything that it represents when it comes to romance. One of my favorite gifts is chocolate — I love it. Flowers are also nice, but there's just something so special about chocolate. Chocolate has a power to captivate unlike any other food. Two of my favorite desserts are Molten Chocolate-Caramel Cake and Chocolate Crème Brûlée.

Grab your favorite chocolate dessert, a comfortable seat and settle down to meet Ransom Winters and Coco Stanley. I enjoyed writing about them and sharing their journey to happily-ever-after with you.

Thanks for the never ending show of support and Happy Valentine's Day.

Jacquelin

CHAPTER 1

"Michael, all that hip-hop music doesn't bother you?" twenty-nine-year-old Constance Stanley asked her brother as they finished packing up a box of chocolates shaped like the Easter Bunny. She was going to drop it off to a preschool down the street from her house later that evening.

The school was having its annual Easter celebration on Friday. Stanley Chocolates donated a box to them every year.

"And if that wasn't bad enough, all I ever see coming out of D-Unit is a bunch of thugs," she complained. "Why didn't the owner just open a music store on Crenshaw or in Compton — anywhere but here in Brentwood?"

"Coco, you worry too much," Michael responded. "There's been no trouble since the store opened, and none of the other tenants are complaining. Have you even gone over there to meet the owner?" Her brother managed their family-owned chocolate factory, Stanley Chocolates, which was next door to her shop.

"No. I'm not sure I want to meet him, either," she huffed. *He's probably a thug as well,* she thought, but didn't say it.

"I think you'd feel better if you do," Michael said as he followed her out to her car. "Instead of making all these snap judgments. C'mon, I'll walk over there with you."

Coco unlocked her door and then shielded her eyes from the bright morning sun. It was a beautiful day in April. Much too pretty to be working inside, but life didn't stop for perfect spring days.

"I don't know . . . maybe later this afternoon," she told him. "That way I can tell him to turn down his music. We definitely don't need him or her scaring away our customers."

Michael laughed. "The music is not that loud, Coco. You can't even understand the lyrics. As for ruining business, I don't think you have to worry about that. You know the saying, 'chocolate is a girl's best friend.' "

"Speaking of chocolate," Coco began, "I have this idea for a new product for my shop. What do you think of combining cardamom, citrus and organic walnuts with

Venezuelan dark chocolate?"

"Sounds delicious," he murmured. "Is this something you want me to experiment with?"

"Actually, I think I'm going to play around with it myself," Coco said with a quick shake of her head. "You have enough to do with that big order that just came in for the Randolph Hotel."

It's not like I have much of a social life these days.

Coco checked her watch. "I need to get out of here. It's almost time for me to open."

Michael gave her a hug. "See you later, sis."

She left the plant and walked next door.

Shortly after Coco opened the doors, her first customer strolled inside.

"Good morning, Stella," she said with a smile.

"Hey, girl," she responded. "Coco, I need half a pound of almond butter crunch."

She quickly packaged the order and handed it to her customer. "It's going to be twenty dollars even."

"Thank you," Stella said. "I just broke up with my boyfriend so I'm curling up tonight when I get home, with a good book and this bag of chocolates. They always make me feel better."

Coco nodded in understanding. There had been many nights when she'd bonded with a bag of chocolate-covered peanuts and a book or a feel-good movie.

Like her brother said, chocolate was a girl's best friend. It was this guilty pleasure that kept her family in business. She had skillfully turned Coco's Chocolate Bar into a very successful venture.

Constance, who preferred to be called by her nickname, Coco, descended from a long line of chocolatiers dating all the way back to the early nineteen hundreds. Her great-great-grandparents had made chocolate and sold it to the local markets. When Coco graduated from college, she'd opted to open a gourmet chocolate shop featuring exotic spices and flavors and make all the chocolate, too, instead of following the family tradition of only making chocolates and distributing them to other stores. Coco had always wanted to open her own specialty shop; it had been a lifelong dream as long as she could remember.

Coco's Chocolate Bar carried exotic chocolates like ones made of sea salt and roasted almonds, pralines and peanuts from Marcona, Spain. Dark chocolates rich with the zip of New Orleans–style chicory coffee and cocoa nibs.

Based in the Brentwood area of Los Angeles, Coco's featured a warm and cozy sitting area, adorned with a beautiful marble bar with mint-green leather chairs for customers to gather and enjoy a taste of her unique chocolates, all of which were produced in the huge plant next door. She also carried her family's line of chocolates.

A young woman strolled into the shop, propelling Coco out of her musings. "Hey you," she said. "Elle, what are you doing here?"

The woman smiled. "I was in the area, so I thought I'd come by and pick up some white-chocolate-covered pralines for Mama. You know how much she loves them."

Coco scooped up the treats into a shiny silver bag. "How is Aunt Amanda doing, Elle? I haven't seen her in months." She tied a mint-green ribbon with brown polka dots around the bag, and then handed it over. She and Elle had been friends since they were both toddlers. Their families were close, so Coco considered them an extended part of her own.

"She's fine," Elle responded. "Just needs to take it easy, but you know how she is — she's not listening to anything her children tell her."

"How are my babies doing?" Coco inquired, referring to Elle's twin boys.

"Great," she answered. "They are not babies anymore, though. They're growing up so fast. I can hardly believe that they're almost four years old."

"That's why you have to enjoy them as much as you can," Coco said. "My niece is turning five on Saturday. I don't know where the time has gone. It seems like it was just a few months ago that I was changing Cinnamon's diapers and giving her a bottle."

Elle sat down in one of the chairs at the bar. "We haven't talked in a while. What's going on with you, Coco? Anyone special in your life?"

"Nope," she answered. "There's no one special. Other than working, there's nothing else going on right now. I'm not complaining, though. I need a little break. Valentine's Day was a bit hectic this year and March was a steady pace. So far April has been good. I expect this weekend to get a little crazy, since it's the Easter weekend."

"I picked up my stuff for the boys' baskets," Elle said. "Now I just need to sit down and do them. Some days I'm just so tired, all I want to do is sleep."

"Are you feeling okay?" Coco asked out of concern.

Elle nodded. "I'm fine. I've put on some weight from all of the eating out and lying around. I think I'm going to go to the gym after Easter." She gestured toward the door. "I see there's a new store across the street. D-Unit? Have you been over there yet?"

Coco shook her head, turning up her nose. "All I ever hear is hip-hop music, so I won't be giving them any of my money. I really wish they had moved to a different location."

"Why?"

She leaned forward, her elbows resting on the bar. "Elle, I moved out here for a reason. See how nice it is? I don't want to be in an area infested with thugs. What do you think that music store is going to bring?" she asked. *"Thugs."*

"What does Michael think? The factory has been in this location for a while."

"My brother thinks I worry too much. I don't think he worries enough."

Elle chuckled. "Sounds like me and my brothers."

"I saw your hubby yesterday. Did he tell you?"

She nodded. "Brennan's leaving to go to Costa Rica on Saturday. He's going to be gone for a week."

Coco eyed her friend. "Why don't you go

with him? You have more than enough people to help with the twins."

"He wants me to, but I don't know."

"Elle, what's up?"

"I just feel that I need to stay home. I don't know what's wrong with me. I'm always tired, it seems, and then Ivy's ex-husband is getting married on Saturday and she's very upset about it, so I think I should stay with her. We're going to take her to a spa that day and then do some retail therapy."

"I remember she was pretty upset over the divorce." Coco shook her head. "I can't believe Charles is getting married again."

Elle nodded. "Ivy kept hoping they would get back together. They had even starting seeing each other last July, and spending time together. Then right after Christmas, Charles announced that he was engaged. Apparently he must have been seeing this girl and Ivy at the same time."

"What a jerk," Coco declared.

Elle agreed, switching her purse from one side to the other. "I'm so disappointed in him."

Coco walked her out to her car. Once outside, she heard music blaring from the center and asked, "Can you hear that craziness?"

"It doesn't sound bad. You just don't care for hip-hop music." Elle listened for a moment. "It's not too loud and you only hear it when the doors open, actually."

"It's a genre of music I wish would just die," Coco uttered. "There's just nothing good about it, in my opinion." She loved classical music, gospel and old school R&B, and truly believed that the world could do without rap music.

"I like some of it," Elle said. "There are a few nice ones out there."

"I really wish the owner had opened at another location. We didn't see all these teenage boys in this area until that store opened. They are over there all the time." Coco's view of teenagers was colored by what she saw and heard on television. So far, she had not met anyone who could refute the images.

Elle embraced her. "It'll work out. Most businesses don't seem to last long over there. That one might be gone before you realize it."

Coco nodded. "You're right about that."

"You should come to Riverside one Sunday for one of the Ransom dinners. We have a great time and I know that Mama would love to see you."

"I'd love to come. Maybe we can do it

one Sunday next month."

Elle smiled. "Look at your schedule and let me know which one you can make."

The two women embraced again.

"Have a great rest of the week."

Coco strolled back into her shop.

The telephone rang.

She knew instinctively that it was her mother calling because she always called around this time. "Coco's Chocolate Bar," she said.

"Good morning, sweetie. It's Mom."

Coco smiled. "I knew it was you. How are you, Mama?" She propped her hip against the mini stainless steel fridge behind the bar.

"I'm fine. Just wanted to check in with you. How is your day going so far?"

"Great," she responded. "Elle was just here."

"I'm having lunch with Amanda on Wednesday. I haven't seen her in a couple of months so we figured it was time for a girls' day out."

"I'm glad you're getting out," Coco said. Her mother hadn't been feeling well due to a bad sinus infection.

"Oh, by the way, Gregory Barton called here. He's in town for the next couple of weeks and wanted to get together with you."

Greg was an old boyfriend from her college days. "What did you tell him?" Coco asked.

"That I'd give you his information. There was nothing else to say."

"So you didn't mention anything about him getting someone else pregnant while he was seeing me?"

"I figured I'd let you handle all of the particulars," her mother said. "I know that you don't like me interfering in your relationships."

Coco laughed. "You are never going to let me forget that, are you?"

"No, I don't think I am," she responded with a short laugh.

A customer walked into the shop.

"Mama, I have to go," Coco said quickly. "I'll call you later."

She silently debated whether or not to give Greg a call. He'd e-mailed her a few times, apologizing for hurting her and for being unfaithful. He had told her that she was the one who had gotten away.

Whatever.

She later decided that it was best to leave the past in the past. She would call Greg back, but only to say goodbye.

Ransom Winters bobbed his head to the

thumping music as he strolled around the room, making sure the boys were completing their school assignments.

Thirty-two years old and a self-made millionaire, Ransom was the founder of D-Unit, a structured day program for at-risk teens who didn't attend school on a regular basis. The boys had a history of excessive class cutting or suspensions in their regular schools; D-Unit was a reputable, short-term alternative for them to attend, but still keep up their regular school assignments.

He paused at the table by a young man wearing a black-and-white Sean John T-shirt. "What are you working on, Jerome?"

The fifteen-year-old glanced up and said, "I have to do a book report on the Civil War."

"Have you started your research?" Ransom asked.

"Not yet." He glanced around the room before adding, "We don't have a computer at home."

"Do you have encyclopedias?"

The boy shook his head, looking embarrassed.

"You can use the computer over there," Ransom said, pointing toward the one on the far left. "We have a set of encyclopedias, as well. Let me know if you need any help."

"Thanks."

Ransom smiled. He truly believed that it took a village to raise children, and having been a youth counselor in the school system, he knew firsthand that most teens weren't misbehaving just because. There was always a reason, usually due to what was going on at home: absent fathers, mothers on drugs, etc. His program allowed teens to come to the center and continue their education. He and his staff worked in a Christian hip-hop environment designed to put the teen boys at ease.

Recent statistics showed that the students in his program returned to school with a change of attitude and grades improved. A couple of the boys had turned in their flags, giving up the gangs to which they once belonged. Before they left the program, Ransom met with each of them to help create short- and long-term goals. He followed up, making regular visits to the schools to make sure his boys were on track and had successfully merged back into the school system.

"I'll be out for a bit," he told one of the staff members. "I'm going to introduce myself to some of the local businesses across the street. Maybe we can find some more volunteer opportunities for the boys. I'll pick up lunch. It's sub sandwiches today. Rick, can you call in their orders for me?"

"No problem," said the man seated over at a desk in the far corner.

Ransom left the center and glanced across the street. He was always looking for ways the boys could perform the community service requirements that were part of his program. He had been considering going over to the Stanley Chocolates factory to see if they would allow his students to come in and work in some capacity for a few hours a day. Many business owners in the small outdoor mall where he was located hadn't been real receptive to having boys with baggy pants and hats on backward in their workplace.

Ransom was never one to give up, so he walked briskly across the street and strode into the plant with purpose.

"May I help you?" the receptionist asked.

"I'd like to speak to the manager, please. I don't have an appointment, so if he or she is busy, I'd like to schedule one. I'm the owner of D-Unit across the street."

She smiled at him. "What is your name, sir?"

"Ransom Winters."

"Michael, there's a Mr. Ransom Winters

here to see you. He's the owner of D-Unit."

She hung up, saying, "Please have a seat. Michael will see you shortly."

"Thank you."

Stanley Chocolates had been around for as long as he could remember. Ransom glanced about the reception area, studying the pictures.

A man walked out from the back. "Hello, I'm Michael Stanley. You're Ransom Winters?"

Rising to his feet, he nodded. "I am." He followed Michael to his office.

Closing the door, Michael said, "I saw a message where you'd called me last week. You were actually on my list to phone today. We had a lot of orders that needed to go out and I was short staffed."

Ransom sat down in the visitor's chair facing Michael. "I completely understand. I really appreciate you seeing me without an appointment." He gave a quick overview of his program.

"I applaud your efforts," Michael responded when he finished his presentation. "I'm sure the response to the center has been overwhelming."

Ransom nodded. "So much that we're opening another one in Inglewood soon. The schools seem to fully be on board. Now

21

if I can just get more of the local businesses to lend their support . . ."

"You can certainly count us in," Michael said. "However, I would like to have an orientation with the boys who will be coming here, and they must adhere to the rules I set for them. If they don't, I will have them leave immediately."

"Understood," Ransom said. "Thanks so much, Michael. I appreciate it, man." He stood up. "I won't keep you from your work any longer. Thanks again."

Michael rose to his feet. "I'll walk you out. By the way, my sister owns the chocolate bar next door. You should go over and introduce yourself. She thought you owned a music store."

"Really?" Ransom asked. "Is the music too loud?"

"I don't really hear it unless your door is open," Michael said. "Nobody's complained, have they?"

"No," he responded. "But I'll cut the volume. I didn't realize you could hear it all the way over here."

A young woman walked into Michael's office just as they shook hands.

"Hey, I was just talking about you," he said to her. "Coco, this is Ransom Winters. He's the owner of D-Unit."

She looked surprised, but recovered quickly and held out her hand. "Hi, I'm Constance, but everyone calls me Coco. It's very nice to meet you."

"The pleasure is all mine," he replied.

Ransom was struck silent by Coco's beauty. He estimated her to be about five-seven. Her body wasn't too thin or too thick — just the perfect size, in his opinion, and her clear complexion was a golden-butternut color. Coco wore her hair in a sassy, short style that gave her a youthful look. He guessed she was in her mid to late twenties.

He finally pulled his attention away from her and glanced at Michael, to find him smiling.

Busted.

He had been caught ogling the man's sister. Hopefully this would not cast him in a bad light. He wanted to leave them with a good impression.

"Sis, I think you need to hear exactly what D-Unit is," Michael told her, sending a wave of relief through Ransom. "It's not what you thought it was."

He smiled at Constance. "I heard that you believed I'd opened a music store. That's not what D-Unit is about."

"I did," she confirmed. "So if you don't

sell music, what do you sell?" Coco scanned his clothing. "Are you selling clothes?"

He shook his head. "I don't sell anything. D-Unit is a center for teens. Right now we're geared to helping boys in particular, but plan to add services for girls by next year. We offer a structured day program."

She regarded him with somber curiosity. "What exactly is that?"

"It's a program designed to help boys stay in school and on target even when they have been suspended."

"So all those teens I've seen coming in and out of your shop are your students?" Coco asked, trying to hide her astonishment. To her they looked more like gang-bangers than students.

"Yes," Ransom answered. "When they're suspended from school, they usually do nothing but run the streets or stay home playing video games. Neither is the best choice for them."

She nodded in agreement. "Wow, you're definitely not a music store. I totally had you figured all wrong."

"I guess with the music always playing, it was natural you made that assumption," Ransom said. "The students seem to relate well to music."

He liked that she seemed interested in his

pilot program. Hopefully Coco would allow one of his boys to put in some volunteer hours at her store. "I haven't been to your shop, but I've heard a lot of good things about it."

"Thank you," she said. "I'm pleased with the way things are going. Word of mouth is the best advertisement."

Michael snapped his finger. "I knew that I recognized your name. You won a Grammy earlier this year."

Ransom smiled and nodded. "Most people have never heard of me." He could feel the heat of Coco's gaze as she quietly observed him.

"You're one of the biggest songwriters out there," Michael said. "I know because I have a couple of friends in the industry. My sister here plays the violin."

Ransom glanced over at her. "I'd love to hear you play sometime."

She gave him a smile that caused his heart to flip. "You might regret it afterward. I haven't played much in years. I've had my hands deep in chocolate."

They laughed.

If her brother had not been standing there, Ransom most likely would've asked Coco out on the spot. But he decided to keep it professional between them. He still held out hope that she would allow one of his students to fulfill his community service hours in her shop. She was one neighbor he was happy to have.

Coco could hardly keep her eyes off the handsome man standing before her. He was not at all what she expected. Ransom had to be at least six-four or -five, his shoulders broad and muscular. His skin was the color of delectable dark chocolate and his eyes a dark brown with a hint of hazel.

He looked familiar, but Coco was sure they had never met. There was something about his eyes. She searched her memory and came up with nothing. She knew some Ransoms but it was their surname.

"I need to get back to the center," he said. "But before I go, I was talking to Michael about community service."

Her brother quickly gave her a recap of their conversation.

"Part of the program includes my students volunteering for community service hours," Ransom interjected.

"I'm going to have some of them help out in the plant," Michael announced.

Guarded, Coco met his gaze. "Really?"

He nodded. "I think it's a good idea, sis."

Although she was very attracted to Ransom, Coco was not about to have a bunch of teens she didn't know working in her shop.

"Would you be interested in having one of my students come in a couple hours a day?"

"I'm sorry, Ransom. My shop brings in a certain type of clientele and, well, I'm not sure how . . ." Coco looked to her brother for help.

Ransom gave her a polite smile. "Thank you for your time. I need to pick up lunch for my students and get back to the center."

"You left me hanging, Michael," she said after Ransom left the plant. "Now he probably thinks I'm nothing but a snob."

"Ransom is doing a good thing with those teens," her brother responded. "It wouldn't have hurt to let one come over to help you."

"I'm not saying it isn't a good program, but he can't change those kids overnight. Michael, you are taking a great risk by bringing them into the plant. You need to discuss this with Dad and see what he thinks."

A flash of anger ignited in Michael's eyes. "I'm the one in control, Coco. I don't need to report to Dad — not about this."

"Those boys lead troubled lives and if they are involved in gangs, who knows what will happen?"

"Maybe all they need is to know that they matter in this world, sis," Michael pointed out. "We grew up with two wonderful parents. Most of those kids are from low-income, single parent homes."

"So you think I'm wrong for not letting them come to my shop?"

He met her gaze. "I never said that, Coco. I can't tell you what to do in your shop."

"And you don't want me telling you what to do in this plant, right?"

"Right," he confirmed. "I have everything over here under control."

Coco released a soft sigh of resignation. "Michael, I hope you know what you're doing."

CHAPTER 2

Ransom was attracted to Coco, but he was disappointed in her stuck-up attitude regarding her clientele. He really hadn't expected her to have any of the students waiting on customers, but she didn't give him a chance to tell her.

He shook his head sadly. He knew too many people like her.

Ransom knew some boys gravitated to gangs because they were looking for something they didn't have at home — a sense of family. But he hated the way people sometimes tended to prejudge teens. There was always a reason for bad behavior, but most adults didn't want to dig deep enough to find it. No one had given up on him, so Ransom vowed to do all he could to help out in turn. He was never going to give up on any child.

Before he ended his canvassing, Ransom picked up two more companies willing to give volunteer hours, so he considered his venture successful. He walked to the deli in the next block to pick up lunch before returning to the center.

Some weeks he had as many as ten boys at D-Unit, but he averaged around four or five. He currently had four students, and decided two would go to the Stanley Chocolates factory, one to the grocery store, and the other would do his community service at the restaurant across the street.

Ransom paid for the sandwiches, chips and sodas. He picked up the box and carried it back to the center. One of his staff members ran out to assist him.

"Thanks," he said.

His eyes traveled over to the fancy lettering in mint green and brown over the door of Coco's shop.

She really was a beautiful woman, Ransom thought to himself. Even if she was stuck-up. Maybe once she got to know him better, he might be able to change her mind about community service for his students.

That wasn't the real reason he wanted to get to know Coco. Ransom couldn't forget that smile she'd awarded him earlier, or the gleam of interest he'd glimpsed in her eyes. They were attracted to each other.

Moving to the Brentwood area had been

one of the best ideas he'd had in a long time.

After a light dinner of spinach salad and grilled salmon, Coco settled down in her den and pulled her violin out of the back of the downstairs closet.

She blew a layer of dust off the instrument.

What am I doing? I haven't played this thing in almost two years. Some fine man tells me that he'd like to hear me play and what do I do? I run home and pull out my violin.

Ransom was just being polite.

I'm doing this for me, she kept telling herself. *It has nothing to do with him.*

Coco made sure to hold the violin properly, with her left arm curved underneath the instrument, the chin rest placed between her left shoulder and jaw. She began playing softly.

She had forgotten how much doing so soothed and calmed her. Coco had been playing the violin since she was ten years old and loved it, although in recent years she'd put it away to focus on building her business.

She drew the bow across the strings, creating a rich, mellow sound. Every now and then she would pluck a string with her index finger, creating a totally different sound. She played until she felt nice and relaxed, then decided to leave the violin out, because she'd really missed playing it.

Still feeling the effects of the busy day, Coco walked through her house to make sure it was secure. Then she headed upstairs to her bedroom and prepared to take a long hot shower.

Her oldest brother, Daniel, called her not too long after. "Are you in bed?" he asked.

"Not yet," Coco answered, putting him on speakerphone while she slipped on her robe.

"I'm not going to keep you, but I promised Grace that I'd call you tonight. She wants to know if you're coming over on Saturday for Cinnamon's birthday party."

Coco smiled at the mention of her niece's name. "Of course I'll be there. Cinna's going to be the big five. I can't miss that."

He gave her the time and location of the party, and then they ended the call.

Coco slipped on a pair of pajamas, then stretched out on the sofa in the sitting room to watch some television before she called it a night. She always watched the news before going to bed.

She frowned. A couple of teenage wannabe gangbangers had attacked a woman, who'd later had a heart attack. She was in the hospital in critical condition.

Coco thought about the types of teens hanging out at D-Unit and felt a growing concern for Ransom. It was admirable how much he wanted to help them, but did those boys really want help? Did they want a better life, and were they willing to work toward it? She wasn't sure, and with all the gang activity spreading, she couldn't help being skeptical.

Her brothers were always after her to stop prejudging before she had all the facts. She didn't have any children, so her only connection was through her friend's children and her niece, who was only four, soon to be five. The only teens that frequented her shop usually came with their parents.

"You can't save the world, Ransom," she whispered.

CHAPTER 3

Coco caught a glimpse of Ransom as he crossed the street with two of his students the next day. She eased over to the window, observing the teenagers. They were dressed in baggy pants and long T-shirts. They looked like thugs to her, but it was clear that Ransom saw something else.

He was talking and laughing with them as if they were all friends. If they were such good kids, then why were they suspended in the first place? Coco wondered.

"I hope Michael knows what he is doing," she whispered, as her mind traveled back to what she'd heard on the news last night. She fervently hoped that her brother wouldn't come to regret his decision.

She considered calling their father, but didn't want to upset Michael. He was running the factory, and would be furious with her if she involved their dad.

Her assistant manager, Valencia, arrived

and walked to the back to clock in for work.

Coco hid her shock when Ransom entered the shop a few minutes later. Smiling, she greeted him cheerfully. "How are you, Ransom?"

"I'm good," he responded, taking a seat at the bar. "I figured since we're neighbors, I should come check out the chocolate here. I've heard a lot of great things about this place."

"So you're coming to see if it lives up to the reviews, huh?"

He met her gaze. "Something like that."

She cleared her throat. "So, how do your students feel about having to work in the factory with Michael?"

"They were actually excited about working with him. I also have one working two doors down at the restaurant, and another at the grocery store."

She frowned. That was not what she'd expected him to say. "Really? They wanted to do it?"

"Yeah, they were eager to work in the factory. I suspect more out of curiosity than anything," Ransom answered. "To be honest, I was surprised Mr. Chou agreed to let me send a kid over. I half expected him to nix the idea."

"He's a nice man and the father of eight,

so he must really love children. I know he does a lot in the community."

"I'd heard that," Ransom told her. "That's why I went to talk to him."

"I know you probably think I'm a snob or something because I refused," Coco stated, folding her arms across her chest. "But I'm really not."

"To be honest, I did think that," Ransom admitted. "But now that I'm seeing this place from the inside, I can tell that you cater to a certain type of customer."

"It's not only that, Ransom. What would I have him do?"

"He could sweep up for you, or wash dishes — anything. He doesn't have to work with your customers."

"I hadn't considered that," she said. "Oh, I'm forgetting my manners. Ransom, would you like something to drink? It's on the house, and hopefully, it'll impress you enough to give a good review when you're asked about the shop."

His smile sent a thrill through her. "Thank you. I'd like to try one of those . . . drinking chocolate. Is that a fancy name for cocoa?"

Coco laughed. " 'Drinking chocolate' is a European term for hot chocolate, Ransom. It's not a powder like cocoa, but actual pieces of chocolate melted into a cup of boiling water or milk. I always use milk."

"So which one would you recommend I try?"

"That will depend on what flavors you like," she answered with a smile. "The dulce de leche is made with real white chocolate and natural caramel." Coco surveyed him for a moment, then said, "You look like a German chocolate kind of man. My German chocolate drink is made of milk chocolate, caramel and coconut milk. Once you take a sip, you'll swear you are back in your grandma's kitchen. I also have strawberries and white chocolate, chocolate mint and Moroccan spice."

"I'll try the German chocolate," Ransom decided.

His cell phone rang.

"Would you excuse me, please? I need to take this call."

While he was talking to someone back at the center, Coco glanced up at him, studying his profile. *This man looks so familiar to me. I must have seen him someplace. But where?* There was something oddly familiar about him, although she was still positive they had never met before now.

She poured the hot liquid into two cups, one for Ransom and one for herself. There was nothing wrong with bonding over a mug of drinking chocolate.

She handed him the cup when he put away his phone.

"Thank you." He took a sip of the soothing liquid and smiled. "You were right. This is delicious and it does remind me of my grandmother's kitchen. She used to make me German chocolate cakes for my birthday every year until the day she died."

"When was that?" Coco inquired.

"Five years ago," Ransom told her. "I miss her a lot. My mom, too."

"You lost your mother?" Coco couldn't imagine the pain of such a deep loss. She adored her mom and didn't know how she would survive such grief.

He nodded. "She died last year."

"I'm so sorry to hear that," Coco said earnestly.

"She worked hard all her life," Ransom murmured. "I'm glad she can rest peacefully now."

"I suppose that's a good way of looking at it." Coco took a sip of her drink, then asked, "Could you please tell me more about your program?"

"Sure," he responded. "What would you like to know?"

"You get these boys only when they're suspended from school, if I understand correctly. I guess I can't help but wonder if what you're doing really helps them in the long term. You only have the students for, what, three or four days?"

"I have them for the entire time they're suspended," stated Ransom. "That can be up to ten days, sometimes longer. And many continue to come back even after they're returned to school."

"Is that enough time to make a real difference in their lives?"

He set his drink down on the bar. "I know we can't save everyone, Coco, but we have had some great successes. I've had two boys give up their flags."

Puzzled, she said, "Give up their flags . . . what does that mean?"

"That they are leaving their gangs," Ransom explained.

"Are they safe when they do that?" Coco asked. "I thought the only way out was through death for most of these kids."

"We move them into a safe house outside of Los Angeles, so that they can live without fear. I have four houses around the country just for situations like this."

She was impressed. "Wow. Ransom, I think that's wonderful. It sounds like you're really dedicated to these boys."

"I am," he confirmed. "I really believe that

it takes a village to raise children, Coco. Most of the students who have come through my program show a marked improvement when they return to school. When they come to me, I get copies of their school records, which show that most are not bad kids. Many are growing up in single parent homes, and gangs provide the family they crave. Some are misjudged because of the way they dress or who they associate with."

"I guess I'm guilty of that," she murmured.

He flashed a winning smile. "It's not too late to change your way of thinking."

"Point taken."

Ransom surveyed his surroundings as he finished his drink. "What are those?" he asked, pointing to the bottles behind the bar.

"Vintage dessert toppings," she responded. "You should try them. I created them by blending wine and chocolate. I have Caramel Chardonnay, Chocolate Raspberry Cabernet, Chocolate Espresso Merlot, Strawberry Champagne and Extreme Dark Chocolate Decadence."

"Now *I'm* impressed," he said. "I'm definitely going to have to try them."

"I hope that you will," she said. Ransom

made her heart skip a beat.

"Coco, I hope I'm not about to make a fool of myself, but would you be interested in having dinner with me tomorrow?"

She released a soft gasp. "You're asking me out? Like on a date?" *Duh . . .*

He nodded.

"Sure," she said. "I'd love to have dinner with you."

He raised his eyes upward. "Thank you, Lord."

She laughed. "Okay, what was that all about?"

"I was giving thanks. I've wanted to ask you out since yesterday, but I wasn't sure what you'd say. I don't even know if you're seeing someone."

"I'm single," Coco assured him. "Since you asked me out, I'm assuming you are, too."

"You assumed correctly."

Coco continued to search her memory, trying to place where she could have seen him. "Ransom, what did you do before taking on the plight of teens?"

"I worked as a high school counselor for three years, and then as a songwriter at a big record label for four years, and I freelanced after that. I guess my name got around and I started writing for some major singers. It's been really good to me. This is why I'm able to start this facility, and I hope to have them all over Los Angeles. I have another one opening soon in Inglewood."

"It sounds like you are truly one of the good guys," Coco told him. "I really hope those boys appreciate what you're doing for them. I certainly do."

"They show me by doing well in school." Ransom checked his watch. "I guess I need to get back to my office. Coco, thanks for the drink and the conversation. I enjoyed both." He pulled out a twenty and handed it to her.

"The drinking chocolate was on the house, Ransom."

"This is a tip." He dazzled her with an incredible sexy smile. "I look forward to our dinner tomorrow night."

She waited until he walked out of the shop before shouting, "Yes!"

Amused, Valencia glanced over at her.

Ransom took Coco to the Jade Empress Pavilion for their first date. She told him she had eaten there once before, but never in one of the private rooms.

"This is nice," she said, her eyes bouncing around the space, which was draped in rich but soothing jewel tones. "All the green foliage and rice paper lanterns really add to the ambience. I feel as if I'm away at an exotic retreat."

"I'm glad you like it," he responded. "I wasn't sure what you'd want to eat, so I might have overordered, but it won't go to waste. I can take whatever we have left to the staff and students on Monday."

They sat down facing each other.

Coco looked stunning in a teal-colored sundress that seemed to love her body, judging by the way the material fell around her hips and flattered her curves.

Waiters started to bring the food out, arranging it attractively on the table.

"We have scallops with a sea garden topping, deep fried stuffed crab claws, Peking duck, Maine lobster, fried rice, and for dessert, mango pudding and Chinese pastries," Ransom told her.

"Wow," she murmured. "I think I'll have a little bit of everything."

"You are a woman after my own heart!" He chuckled and picked up the chopsticks.

"Are you really going to eat with those things?" Coco asked.

"Aren't you?"

She shook her head. "Oh no, that's not part of my skill set."

"You have to try it," Ransom said.

"C'mon, I'll help you. Just watch me and then you do it."

Coco put forth a valiant effort to eat with chopsticks, but ended up laughing at herself. "Okay, I give up. I'm using my fork or I won't be able to enjoy dinner."

"You were doing fine."

"Yeah, right," she said, pointing to the stain on his silk shirt. "That's why you're wearing some of our dinner. Seriously though, I'm real sorry about that and I'll be more than happy to pay for the cleaning."

Ransom waved away her concern. "Don't worry about it."

Coco stuck a forkful of lobster in her mouth, savoring the flavor. "This is delicious."

"Have you tasted the duck?" he asked.

"I'm trying it now." She sampled the tender meat and nodded in approval. "It's really good."

Coco took a sip of her iced water. "So tell me something," she said. "Why are you always playing rap music? Most of that stuff degrades women and glorifies gang life, right? I would think that it goes against what you stand for."

"Have you listened to the lyrics?" he inquired.

"Not really," she admitted. "I can't stand

hip-hop, so I don't really pay attention to it. I'm more of a classical music and old school R & B kind of girl."

"I think you should be more open-minded when it comes to music, Coco. All you heard coming from the center was hip-hop and you immediately assumed it was bad. You didn't even bother listening to the lyrics. If you had, you would have realized that it was gospel or Christian hip-hop. I don't know if you've realized this but classical music has been sampled in several hip-hop songs," Ransom explained. "Nas skimmed from Beethoven's 'Für Elise.' Young Buck used beats from Mozart's *Requiem.* Ludacris snagged from both *Requiem* and Dvořák's *Symphony No. 9.*"

"I didn't know that," Coco said. "That's pretty interesting — this whole hip-hop, classical combination."

They continued to talk about music while they finished their meal.

Afterward, Ransom drove her home. Since it was their first date, he didn't want to keep her out too late and sought to end the night on a high note.

She was still on his mind when he pulled into the garage at his home in Santa Monica.

Coco had a wonderful sense of humor.

45

He had enjoyed the evening with her. Ransom smiled as he recalled how clumsy she was with chopsticks. She'd been laughing so hard at her inability that the results had been disastrous. He glanced down at his stained silk shirt. It was ruined, so he decided to toss it. The evening had been worth it, however. Ransom was looking forward to seeing Coco again.

Coco had misjudged Ransom completely.

He was a really nice person who cared deeply for youth in the community. He was also a lot of fun, she admitted to herself.

He certainly is a good sport. I don't think I'd be that nice if someone ruined my silk blouse.

Okay, so I know I wouldn't be as magnanimous.

Coco loved the way his kissable lips parted when he laughed that deep, throaty laugh. He was a very handsome and sexy man. She thought about the sensual product line in her store. She'd sold quite a few of the items, but had never tried them herself. She really wanted to try the body frosting, since she had received such rave reviews on it.

Okay, so I'm totally in lust over this man. Maybe I should go take a cold shower.

It had been months, maybe even a year, since she had been involved in a serious relationship. The older she became, the quicker she was able to detect the jerks, and since she refused to settle, Coco was still single.

She was not a woman who believed she needed a man in her life, but it didn't mean she wanted to be alone, either. She was ready for that special someone, but he had to come with the whole package.

Her ideal man was family oriented, had a strong work ethic and great sense of humor, and would love her with his whole heart.

Her mind traveled back to Ransom.

"Cold shower, here I come," she said with a groan.

The next day Coco got up early and drove the short distance to the shop to work on a special treat for her niece. The store was busy because it was the day before Easter Sunday. All of her employees were there and things appeared to be going smoothly.

She didn't leave until shortly after two. She talked with her assistant manager and another employee before saying, "I'll see you all on Monday. Happy Easter."

"Thanks for the Easter baskets," Valencia told her.

Coco had made one for each of her employees. "You're quite welcome."

She walked outside and quickly made her

way to her car.

Singing softly with the music, Coco merged onto the 405 freeway, going south. Her brother and his family lived in Marina Del Rey.

"Auntie Coco, you're here," Cinnamon exclaimed when she arrived forty-five minutes later. "What took you so long?"

"I'm sorry for being late. There was a car accident on the way over here and traffic was backed up, honey." The trip normally took her less than thirty minutes.

The little girl hugged her. "I'm so glad that you're here now. We're gonna have lots of fun."

"We sure are," Coco said.

She waved at her brothers and her parents as Cinnamon led her over to the table where the birthday cake was on display.

"Look, Auntie . . . I have a Barbie doll cake."

"I can see that," Coco responded. "It's beautiful."

"We're gonna have hot dogs and hamburgers."

"Yum."

"Auntie, did you make me a special chocolate for my birthday?" Cinnamon asked eagerly.

Every year Coco created a special bag of

chocolates for her niece. She pulled out a silver bag now. "How about some white chocolate and orange crème delight?"

"Oooh, that sounds delicious." Cinnamon held out her hand. "Can I please try some of them now?"

"You have to ask your parents," she replied. "But you know what I think?"

"What?"

"These will taste better after you've had a hot dog or a hamburger. This will trigger the yum-yum buds."

"Really?" Cinnamon asked, her big brown eyes wide. "A hot dog can do *that?*"

Coco bit her bottom lip to keep from laughing. "S-sure can, honey."

"I'm gonna go get one now. I might eat a hamburger, too. I'll get lots of yum-yum buds then."

"Sounds like a plan to me," she told her niece.

"Liar liar pants on fire," Michael said from behind her.

She turned around. "See, that's why you're not married."

He chuckled. "Why? Because I won't tell lies? You're probably right. Honesty certainly hasn't gotten me any closer to the altar."

Coco feared she had hurt his feelings

somehow, so she said, "Michael, I was kidding."

"I know that, sis. I think there may be some truth to it, though. You know what my date told me last night? She actually said that I was too nice."

Coco felt a rush of anger. "What?"

Michael shrugged nonchalantly. "Any woman who needs a little thug in her life definitely isn't the one for me."

"She actually told you that?" Coco asked. "That's the stupidest thing I've ever heard."

He nodded in agreement. "I couldn't get away from her quick enough."

Coco looped her arm through her brother's. "Well, it's just you and me."

"Not anymore," Michael responded with a grin. "You're hanging out with Ransom these days. How did your date go?"

"I ruined his silk shirt," she announced. "But other than that, everything went well, I thought."

"How did you mess up the man's shirt?"

"I was trying to eat with chopsticks and, well, the food sort of flew away and landed on his chest. I really was aiming for my mouth."

Michael cracked up laughing. "Stay away from chopsticks, Coco."

"You don't have to worry about that," she

said. "I'm amazed the man wants to go out with me again."

"Me, too," Michael said.

Coco jabbed him in the arm.

She heard Cinnamon calling her name and said, "I guess we'd better get back there and do the auntie-uncle thing."

"Let's do it," Michael said.

CHAPTER 4

On Monday Coco walked over to D-Unit with a gift for Ransom. She had ruined his shirt so she went out first thing that morning to buy him another one. Coco had found one that was pretty close to the color he'd worn the other night, purchased it and had it wrapped.

He currently had three students, who were sitting at desks working on class assignments or homework. They seemed busy and focused, and she regretted disturbing them by her arrival.

Ransom ushered her into his office.

"How was your Easter?" she asked, taking a seat on the sofa.

He sat down beside her. "It was good. I went to sunrise service and then had breakfast with my pastor and his wife. How about yours?"

"My brothers and I all attended church with our parents and had dinner together afterward." *I thought about you all day long and how much I enjoyed our dinner together.*

"I bought this for you," Coco said. "I felt really bad for ruining your shirt."

"You didn't have to do this," Ransom told her.

"I did," she replied. "That shirt was very expensive and I'm pretty sure it was ruined. The one I bought isn't quite the same color, but it's close."

He opened the box. "Coco, I actually like this color much better." Ransom leaned over and kissed her. "Thank you."

She resisted the urge to touch the place where his lips had been. Her heart was racing and Coco could feel her blood rushing through her veins. She hadn't known Ransom a week yet and she was already falling for the man.

"Coco . . ."

She glanced at him. "I'm sorry. Did you say something?"

"I didn't offend you just now, did I?"

"No, you didn't," she answered. "Not at all. To be honest with you, I loved it and would do it again."

Whoa. Slow down.

Coco took a deep breath, then exhaled. "I can't believe I just rambled on like that."

"You didn't ramble. In fact, I enjoyed

hearing it and would love to kiss you again."

Laughing, she boldly met his gaze. "What are you waiting for?"

His mouth covered hers hungrily.

A knock on the door had them scrambling for air.

Ransom rushed to his feet and said, "Come in."

One of the teens peeked inside. His eyes darted back and forth between Coco and Ransom suspiciously for a moment.

"What do you need, Benjamin?"

"Uh . . . Mr. Winters, I wanted to let you know that I finished my math. Can I get on the computer? We're supposed to get the information on the history projects. Since I'm not there, I wanted to see if she posted it on the Web site."

Ransom nodded. "That's fine, Benjamin. I'll be out there in a few minutes to check your math assignment."

His eyes traveled once more to Coco and his mouth curved upward. "I'm sorry for disturbing y'all."

"It's all right," Ransom said. "Back to work, Benjamin."

"I just want to say one thing, Mr. Winters. You got great taste." Grinning from ear to ear, the teen closed the door and was gone.

"Wow," Coco said with a smile. "He's

good for my self-esteem."

"Benjamin is a good kid. His father left when he was six years old. He's the oldest of four and his mother is sick. He works nights and takes care of the family."

"He's how old?"

"Sixteen. He'll be seventeen next week. He's here because he mouthed off at one of his teachers, who was ragging him about homework."

"Does she know all this?"

Ransom shook his head. "She's never asked Benjamin about his life. She's never inquired why sometimes he falls asleep in class or doesn't have all of his homework done. She assumes that he's just lazy and doesn't want to be in school. She has no idea that Benjamin sees getting into college as his only way to a better life for him and his family."

"Does he have the grades to get into college?"

"He could," Ransom said. "He's certainly smart enough. He is a phenomenal basketball player, too, but because he has to work and doesn't get off until midnight, he has no time for sports or any other school activities."

"Is there anything that can be done to help him?" Coco asked. "He needs to be able to focus on his academics if he wants to get into college. What does he want to study?"

"Mechanical engineering."

Her eyes widened in surprise. "Really?"

"He can do it," Ransom said. "I'm looking into what services are available to help his family. I'm also trying to figure out a way for him to make some decent money and not have it interfere with his schoolwork. I'm afraid he'll start looking for ways to make a lot of money in a short period of time, and if that happens . . ."

"I don't even want to think about it," Coco said. "Wait a minute! Maybe Michael can help. Benjamin could work at the plant after school and on the weekends, but he'd still be able to get off in time to do homework and spend time with his family. I'm sure we pay more than what he's making right now."

"He makes minimum wage."

"Yeah, we definitely pay more than that. Let me talk to Michael and I'll give you a call later."

Coco was about to walk out of the door, but Ransom pulled her back into his arms and kissed her.

She returned his kiss with a hunger that belied her outward calm. Burying her face

56

in his neck, Coco breathed a kiss there.

"I'd better get out of here while I still can," she whispered. "I want to catch Michael before he leaves. He has a meeting sometime this afternoon."

"Thank you," Ransom said when they parted. "Benjamin deserves every chance he can get."

Coco waited for her breathing to return to normal. "I'll call you after I speak with my brother."

An hour later, she and Michael walked back over to D-Unit.

Ransom met them at the door.

"Coco told me about Benjamin," her brother told him. "I'd like to speak with him, if you don't mind."

"You can use my office."

While they were in the back talking, Ransom introduced Coco to the other teens and his staff.

"You the lady that owns the chocolate bar over there?" the one named Jerome asked.

"Yes, I am," she said.

"I bet you have some real expensive candy in there — it looks like it from the outside. I only peeked in once and I felt like I couldn't afford to even walk in the place."

Coco wasn't sure how to respond to his comment.

"I like to see my people do good," he told her. "It inspires me."

She smiled. "Jerome, what is it that you'd like to do?"

"Stay alive, for one thing, and then go to college so that I can have my own business one day."

"From what I'm seeing, you are on the right track, Jerome."

He gave her a genuine smile.

Coco turned to Ransom and said, "I know what's missing over here. You need chocolate. Michael and I will get together and send over a nice selection of chocolate snacks."

Before he could respond, her brother and Benjamin strolled out of Ransom's office. From the big grin on the teen's face, Coco knew that Stanley Chocolates had a new employee.

She wished there was something more she could do to help Benjamin.

Ransom took Coco to a Christian hip-hop concert on their second date. Initially, she wasn't thrilled with the idea, but as she listened to the words, she found herself warming up to the music.

Coco could tell that Ransom was thoroughly enjoying himself. He caught her watching him and flashed her that sexy smile that caused a shudder to pass through her. When she closed her eyes, she could see him covered in body frosting lying in the middle of a bed.

Oh no, I'm at a Christian concert. Please forgive me, Lord. Okay, I need to really get a grip on this lusting.

Coco crossed her legs and focused on the music. She didn't dare look at him until it was time for them to leave.

"So what did you think?" he asked her afterward.

"Huh? Oh, I had a great time," Coco told him. "I actually surprised myself because I really enjoyed the music."

He broke into a grin.

"Okay, you were right. There, I've said it."

"Hey, I'm just glad you had a good time," Ransom stated. "Coco, thank you for coming with me. I didn't want to go alone. Concerts are no fun when you're by yourself, in my opinion."

I'd go anywhere with you. Well, not really anywhere, but most places.

She caught Ransom staring at her. "What is it?"

"Sometimes you have this look of pure amusement. It's as if you're hearing something no one else can hear."

Man, he's good.

"No, it's not that," Coco said. "Ransom, we've only known each other for a very short time, but there are moments when I feel as if I've known you forever."

He nodded. "I feel the same way. Maybe it's because I really enjoy your company."

She smiled.

"Coco, I'm not a man to beat around the bush. I'm very interested in you and I would like to pursue a relationship with you. I'd like to see where this road takes us."

"I feel the same way," she said.

"Then that means another date has to follow, hence the whole dating thing."

"Just tell me when and where," Coco responded with a chuckle. "Actually, I have it. Ransom, my parents are having a dinner party on Saturday for some of our VIP clients. I'd like for you to be my date."

"I wouldn't have it any other way," he said.

Ransom met Coco at her parents' Century City home. She had gone over there earlier to help her mother with last-minute details.

A woman dressed in a black-and-white uniform greeted him and directed him to the back of the house, where everyone was gathering. As he passed by the kitchen, the smell of freshly sautéed garlic and herbs tantalized his senses, causing his stomach to growl in protest.

Coco saw him and navigated through the sea of guests toward him. "I'm glad you made it. My mom's dying to meet you."

"Where is she?" he asked.

"She went upstairs for a moment, but she'll be back."

Ransom chuckled. He silently noted the muted gold walls and deep emerald green tones displayed throughout the furnishings. He was still in the process of decorating his new house, so he looked to pick up tips wherever he could.

Coco led him over to her father.

"This is my date, Ransom Winters."

"It's nice to meet you, son." After a brief pause, he added, "I apologize for staring. You look familiar to me and I was trying to figure out if we'd met before. So your name is Ransom Winters, huh?"

"I'm afraid we haven't met until now, although I grew up with Stanley Chocolates," Ransom said.

"Well, it's a pleasure to have met you, Ransom. A real pleasure."

There was something in the elder Stanley's eyes — a flash of recognition. . . . *What was that about?* Ransom wondered briefly. He gazed around the room, taking in the dining guests and the ambience.

Coco introduced him to her brother Daniel and his wife. Then her mother approached them. "This must be Ransom," she said.

"He is," Coco replied. "This is my mother, Eleanora Stanley."

"It's nice to meet you, Mrs. Stanley."

Smiling warmly, Eleanora nodded in approval. "He's a very handsome man, Coco."

"Thanks for pointing that out, Mama." Coco took him by the hand and said, "Will you please excuse us?"

Ransom burst into laughter. "I like your mom."

"Yeah, I guessed you would."

A waiter walked up to them carrying a tray of wineglasses. Ransom took one and handed it to Coco. He then got one for himself.

"Just so you know, my mother is not ashamed of her quest to have me married and pregnant. She fully believes that I should have a husband and that Michael needs a wife. Actually, I think my brother needs one, too."

"So you're not looking to get married?" Ransom murmured. He was more than ready to settle down himself and start a family. It was all he really wanted in life, since he had achieved everything else.

"I'd like to get married one day," Coco admitted. "I'm just not obsessing over it."

Everyone gathered under the huge white tent that had been set up in her parents' backyard. After her father said grace, the guests formed lines for the buffet.

"Everything on the menu is delicious," Coco whispered to Ransom. "But one of my personal favorites is the prawns with sun-dried tomatoes, roasted peppers and spinach. The other is the lobster tail soaked in a lemon-butter sauce. And the baked chicken is really good. We use this catering company all the time. If you're ever looking for a caterer, you should try them."

Ransom filed that piece of information in the back of his mind.

They sat down at the table that had been reserved for them.

He sampled the food. "I'll definitely give these folks a call when I'm looking for a caterer," he told Coco.

Her smile warmed him. Ransom had no idea why Coco affected him the way she did, but instead of dwelling on the thought, he pushed it to the back of his mind and prepared to enjoy the rest of the evening.

CHAPTER 5

Jerome surprised her when he walked through the doors of her shop. Coco checked the clock and noted that it was after three.

"I just stopped in to say hello before I took the bus home," he told her.

"How was your day?" she asked.

"Okay," he responded with a shrug. "I got all of my class work done and I'm almost done with my homework."

Coco smiled. "That's great, Jerome."

She watched as he walked around the store, looking at everything, but touching nothing.

He turned to her and said, "Miss Stanley, since I met you and your brother, I . . . I started reading up on making chocolate."

She was surprised by this. "Really?"

He nodded. "I wanted to know what all it took to make it. I didn't know that you had to roast cocoa beans."

"It's a long process," Coco told him. "But before you even get to that point, the beans have to ripen and that usually takes five to six months. Then they have to be fermented."

"Why do you do that?" he asked.

"To make them less bitter and to darken the color." Coco went on to explain that after fermentation, the beans were sun-dried for several days to bring out the aroma, then packed and shipped to factories that would sort and clean the beans. "Roasting the beans helps the flavor come through," she finished.

"I like knowing how things work," Jerome stated.

"It's good to have a curious mind," Coco responded. "I was like that in school. Actually, I'm still that way." She paused for a moment. "Jerome, can I ask how you ended up suspended from school?"

"Miss Stanley, I have a sister. She and I are twins, and there's this dude at school who's been pushing up on her. Jeri doesn't like him like that, but he keeps trying to get with her. Anyway, he had her in the gym and was trying to force himself on her. I couldn't let nothing like that go down, so I jumped the dude." His hands curled into fists as he talked. "I'm not gon' let some dude rape my sister."

"And they suspended you for that?"

He nodded. "They suspended the dude, too, because we were fighting."

"Didn't you tell them what happened? What about your sister? Did she come forward?"

"Miss Stanley, they don't care. All they see is a black boy who lives in a place they never been."

"Jerome, I hope you know you're much more than that. You have a curious mind that needs to be fed. I know there are teachers in schools who are doing more harm than good, but it's up to you. You have to take control of your education."

"How can I do that?"

"First, let me say that I don't believe you should've been suspended. You were trying to save your sister and I find that admirable. Before this, what were your grades like?"

"I got two A's, two B's, one C and a D last semester."

"That's not bad, but I have a feeling you can do much better."

"I could, but I don't have a computer at home," Jerome said. "We don't have any encyclopedias either. For some of my stuff, I need a computer. Both my math and science books are on a CD. I can't study at home."

"Do you live near a library?"

"Not really," he responded. "But Mr. Winters told me that I can come to the center after school and do my homework."

Coco walked around the bar and sat down in one of the chairs. She gestured for Jerome to sit beside her. "Are you struggling with any of your subjects?"

"Just math, but Mr. Winters is going to tutor me so I can pull up from a D."

"What classes were the two A's from?" Coco asked.

Jerome smiled. "One was in P.E. and the other in history. I love history, especially African-American history."

"I love African-American history myself. In fact, I recently acquired a couple of copies of *The Underground Railroad Records* by William Still. It chronicles the runaway slaves who traveled the Underground Railroad to freedom."

Jerome's eyes lit up like stars in the sky. "Man, that's nice. I'd love to read that."

Coco gazed at him. "If I gave you a copy, would you read it and take care of it? It's a rare edition now."

He blinked twice. "Miss Stanley, I'd treat it like gold. It's our history. You don't just throw it away — even though *they* tried to dismiss all we've done. I want that book to stay in my family and be passed down to my children. I can't believe you'd give something like that to me."

The expression on his face almost brought Coco to tears. "As you said, this is our history."

She got up, walked back around the bar and reached under the counter. "Jerome, this is yours," Coco told him. "As you read these stories, purpose in your heart that you're not going to let what those people fought so hard for just fall to the wayside."

A tear slipped from his eye. "Miss Stanley, you don't know what this . . . how much this means to me. You and Mr. Winters — y'all are some really good people. You care. I ain't never . . . I haven't had that. I'm not gonna let ya'll down."

She wiped away her own tears. "Jerome, I want you to care, even when you feel others don't. You have to care what happens, and strive to be the best you can be."

He nodded.

"I look forward to hearing great things about you in the future." She pointed to a machine and asked, "Would you like a cold chocolate soda?"

Jerome gave her a sheepish look and said,

"I don't have any money."

His stomach growled loudly then.

"I was just about to eat my sandwich and I have an extra one," Coco said. "How about you have a late lunch with me? It's my treat."

"Miss Stanley . . . you don't have to do tha—"

She cut him off. "Great! I hate to eat alone."

He laughed.

They made small talk while they ate. Afterward, Jerome said, "Where's your broom? I'ma sweep up before I head home."

Coco pointed to the small closet in the corner. "It's in there. Thanks, Jerome."

"I just want to show my appreciation," he said.

Coco watched him grab the broom and begin sweeping. Jerome was thorough. He didn't rush, but took his time, making sure that he didn't leave an inch of flooring untouched.

Ransom strode into the shop with purpose, pausing briefly when he saw Jerome. "Hey, man, I thought you had gone home."

"He stopped in to say hello and we got to talking," Coco interjected. "Then we had lunch and he offered to sweep up."

Ransom went over and patted him on the shoulder, saying, "Jerome, I'm proud of you."

The teenager shrugged. "She's real nice and I wanted to do something for her."

Ransom sat down at the bar. "Exactly what happened here between you two? I haven't seen Jerome this engaged since he started the program. I can hardly get him to talk."

"He told me why he was suspended," she responded in a low voice. "Which I think is wrong on so many levels, Ransom. He should not be suspended. Jerome was only defending his sister."

"I agree with you, but the school feels that he should have just reported it to campus security."

"He seems to be a good kid," she said. "I admit that I didn't get it at first, but now I really understand why you're so passionate. Boys like Jerome and Benjamin deserve to have every opportunity available to them."

Ransom was staring at her, sending a delicious shudder through her body.

"What is it? Why are you staring at me like this?"

"I can't get over how beautiful you are," he said, bringing a smile to her lips.

"You do know that we're not alone, Ransom."

"Jerome knows that you're beautiful." Ransom glanced over his shoulder, then said, "You know, I really think he has a little crush on you. I'm going to have to keep my eye on him, I see."

Coco rolled her eyes. "I think Jerome just wants to be around people he feels he can trust."

Ransom considered her words for a moment before shaking his head. "That's probably true, but I think he also has a crush on you. I can't blame him, though. You've mesmerized me."

CHAPTER 6

"How long has your friend been playing the violin?" Ransom asked her.

"Since she was four years old," Coco responded. "I went to a recital to hear her play and that's when I decided I wanted to take lessons. Ariel is amazing."

"So when do I get to hear *you* play?" he asked.

"Soon," she told him.

Ransom had mentioned on several occasions that he wanted to hear Coco play the violin. He had no idea, but she was going to play a solo tonight. Ariel already had her instrument on stage. Coco had been practicing every night for the past couple of weeks.

Please don't let me go up there and make a fool of myself. I want to impress him with my moves.

The thought made her chuckle.

"What's so funny?" Ransom whispered in her ear.

"I just had a silly thought," she whispered back. "It's nothing."

The heavy velvet curtains parted and classical music filled the stage and hall. Coco glanced at Ransom, who was slightly swaying his head back and forth. He must have felt her looking at him because he turned to face her.

When he reached over and took her hand, his touch set her nerve endings on fire.

I've got to stop this, she told herself as her heart hammered foolishly.

She stole another glance at him, noting how handsome he looked in the black suit he was wearing. It fit his body as if it had been designed just for him.

This man is so fine.

Coco was totally entranced by his compelling personage and had to struggle to keep her attention on the music. Ariel walked out to roaring applause to perform her first solo. She would be calling Coco to join her after her third selection.

Ransom gave her hand another little squeeze. Coco's flesh prickled at his touch and her heart was hammering foolishly.

Focus. Focus.

It's what she kept telling herself, but doing so wasn't that simple. Ransom made her feel things she'd never experienced before. Or maybe she was just out of touch with those particular emotions, since she hadn't been in a relationship in a while.

It was almost time for her performance.

Coco felt a wave of nervousness.

Maybe this wasn't such a good idea, after all. She prayed she wouldn't embarrass them both.

Ransom was shocked when Ariel called Coco to the stage.

He met her gaze, then smiled. "You planned this, didn't you?" he whispered.

"You said that you wanted to hear me play."

Ransom was touched by her gift to him.

Coco looked beautiful up there on stage, as if she belonged there. His heart did flips when she dedicated to him the song she was about to play. She projected an energy and power that undeniably attracted him.

Coco played a classical number, then segued into a song that he had written. He enjoyed watching her become one with the music. Ransom had made millions writing songs for various recording artists, and owned several Grammys. He liked the way she had successfully arranged the solo, bringing classical music and a classic R&B song together.

Afterward, he met her backstage.

"So what did you think?" Coco asked him.

Every time her gaze met his, Ransom's heart turned over in response. "You did a fabulous job."

"I agree," Ariel said, joining them. "She should be on stage performing."

"Ariel, this is Ransom," Coco said. "He's my date."

She shook his hand. "I've heard a lot about you. It's nice to finally put a face to the name."

"I enjoyed your music, Ariel."

"Thank you." She gave Coco a hug and said, "I'm going to have to get going. I'm catching the red-eye to New York and then on to Germany."

"Ariel's booked to play for our troops at Ramstein Air Force Base," Coco told him.

"Safe travel," Ransom said. "I know they are going to enjoy hearing your music. I have a couple of friends stationed there."

"I'll call you when I return," she said to Coco before heading to her dressing room. "Smooches."

Ransom and Coco headed toward the nearest exit doors, and were soon in the car and on their way to her house in Brentwood. He glanced over at her. She had her eyes closed.

"I'm not asleep," she said. "I'm just trying to relax enough to get over my performance jitters. I was so nervous up on that stage."

He was completely surprised by this. "You were nervous? I couldn't tell."

"Oh, my goodness," Coco groaned. "Right now I feel so nauseous. It'll pass in a few minutes. I used to get this way after every recital or concert."

Ransom slipped in a soothing jazz CD, hoping to help her feel at ease. She sent him a grateful smile.

Coco had such a warm, loving spirit and she was always smiling. He loved her sometimes quirky sense of humor, and the sense of freedom she seemed to have in her life. Not only was she beautiful, but she was intelligent and caring as well. The more he got to know her, the more he wanted to know about her. An undeniable magnetism was building between them, forcing him to acknowledge the truth.

I have real feelings for this woman, and I can't see my life without her in it.

The silent declaration surprised him, but Ransom didn't bother to deny the truth.

"What do you think about this one?" Elle asked, holding up a matronly black dress.

Coco glanced at Kaitlin, who shook her

head. "I don't think Brennan will like it."

Coco met Elle's gaze and said, "I have to agree with her. It looks a little old-fashioned. I wouldn't get it."

"I thought it was cute."

"What's going on with you, Elle?" Kaitlin asked. "Why are you suddenly wanting to dress like a nun? All you've been wearing lately are these loose dresses and big shirts."

"I've gained some weight," she said, sounding embarrassed. "I'm getting a belly, and look at my face."

Kaitlin and Coco exchanged glances.

"What?" Elle asked, looking from one to the other.

"Sweetie, did it ever occur to you that you might be pregnant?" Coco asked.

"No, not really," responded Elle. "I . . . I've been so busy that I haven't thought about that possibility."

Kaitlin nodded. "I think Coco's right. Elle, you're pregnant."

She placed a hand to her stomach. "Brennan and I just talked about having another baby. I made a doctor's appointment for next week to get checked out."

"Let's get a pregnancy test," Kaitlin suggested.

"Now?" Elle asked.

"Yeah. We're not that far from your house.

We can go there and in a few minutes have your answer."

"Coco, you're coming with us, right?" Elle inquired.

"Sure."

They left the boutique and piled into Elle's car.

They stopped at a nearby drugstore to purchase a pregnancy test, then headed to her house.

Elle went into the bathroom to take the test as soon as they entered. "I'll be back in a sec," she said.

"So you and Brennan were planning to have another baby?" Kaitlin asked when Elle joined them in the family room.

"Yeah, we wanted to try for one more." She paced back and forth across the floor nervously, her eyes darting to the clock on the wall. "I thought I was putting on extra pounds because all I've done lately is eat, sleep and watch TV. I'm exhausted all of the time."

"That's because you're pregnant," Coco said.

She wanted to have children one day, but needed to find a husband first. She thought about Ransom and smiled.

"It's time," Elle said. She picked up the test and stared at it. "Oh, my goodness," she murmured softly.

"Don't keep us in suspense," Kaitlin cried. "Are you pregnant? C'mon, tell us what it says."

"I'm pregnant," Elle announced, her eyes bright with joy. "I'm going to have a baby."

Coco got up and hugged her. Kaitlin hugged her next.

"You're going to be a mom again. That's so wonderful. Congratulations!"

"Brennan is going to be so surprised."

"Matt wants another baby," Kaitlin said.

Elle and Coco looked at her. "And?" they asked in unison.

"We're still in the talking stages. I'm thirty-four years old."

"You're not too old," Elle told her. "But if you keep waiting, then you will be."

"I can't wait to get married and have babies," Coco said. "I hope when I finally find Mr. Right that he's ready to have children. I don't want to wait too long."

The trio left the house and drove to one of Elle's favorite restaurants to have a celebratory lunch.

"I bet this happened the night we tried your chocolate lovers dice game," Elle told Coco.

"What chocolate lovers dice game?" Kaitlin asked.

Elle leaned forward and said, "Girl, you have to get one. You roll the dice and he has to interpret your wish. It's a lot of fun."

"Apparently," Kaitlin murmured.

"I thought I told you about the game," Coco said. "It comes with a bottle of choco-holics body frosting, five colored dice, wish interpretation cards and a soft paintbrush."

"I'm coming by the store to pick up one of those," Kaitlin stated. "Matt and I are going away this weekend for romance — this is perfect."

Elle laid down her menu. "Coco, you have all those sensual chocolate treats in your shop — c'mon, who are *you* using them with?"

"I'm not using them," she replied. "Believe me, I'm dying to try them out. I've just started seeing this guy, but it's way too early to start using body frosting and paint-brushes. Oh, by the way, his first name is Ransom and he's the owner of D-Unit."

"The music store?" Elle asked. "Just a few weeks ago you couldn't stand the guy."

"It's not a music store," Coco explained. "It's actually a center for teenage boys. Ransom calls it a structured day program. When they're suspended from school, they go there during the school hours instead of just sitting at home or running the streets.

He has their home and class assignments e-mailed to him, so that they can stay on task."

"That's wonderful," Elle said. "I've never heard of a program like that, but I think we need more like it."

"It's a pilot program. Ransom hopes that he'll have centers all over Los Angeles. He also wants to add programs for girls."

Kaitlin observed her for a moment before saying, "Sounds like you two are really getting along well. You're actually glowing, Coco."

"I don't know about that," she said.

Elle took a sip of her water. "Why don't you just admit it? You like this guy a lot. Don't you?"

Coco couldn't deny it. "Is it that obvious?" she asked.

Kaitlin and Elle both nodded.

"Do you think Ransom knows?"

They nodded a second time.

"I'm falling hard for him," Coco confessed. "But we haven't been dating that long."

"Love knows no time," Kaitlin said. "I fell in love with Matt the moment I saw the man."

"It was like that for me and Brennan," Elle interjected. "Hopefully you won't have the

81

baby mama drama that I had to deal with."

"He doesn't have any children," Coco said. "Although he's always surrounded by youths who look to him as a father figure. He really cares about them."

"So when do we get to meet Mr. Wonderful?" Elle demanded.

"You know how I am," Coco said with a chuckle. "It'll probably be at the wedding. If there's no wedding, then that means he wasn't worth introducing to family and close friends."

Kaitlin and Elle laughed.

CHAPTER 7

Coco attended Jerome and Benjamin's graduation on Friday. Their suspensions over, they would be returning to their school on Monday.

"I wish that we could just come here for school," Jerome said as he stood up at the podium. "None of my teachers there showed me any interest like Mr. Winters and everyone here." His eyes traveled to where Coco was sitting. "Miss Stanley over there told me that I have to take ownership of my education, and that's what I'm going to do." He pointed to the principal and guidance counselor who were in attendance. "I was wrong for fighting, but I was protecting my sister. I was wrong and I apologize for the way I handled the situation. I'm in school to get an education."

Jerome met their gazes. "I want that. I want to go to college, and starting today, I'm not going to let anyone stop me."

His principal surprised everyone when he stood up and clapped. "Son, we are there to help you get that education. If you find we are lacking in some way, you come to me."

"Do you think he means it?" Coco asked in a low whisper.

"I hope so, but don't worry," Ransom whispered back. "I'm going to be tracking Jerome. If there's a problem, I'll step in."

Benjamin walked up to the podium.

"I feel the same way Jerome does. None of my teachers ever cared why I fell asleep in class or didn't get my homework finished. They never asked me anything. They didn't know that I worked forty hours a week to support my family because my mother has cancer. She can't work." His eyes teared up and his voice broke. "She couldn't come here today because chemo makes her really sick. Mr. Winters checked around and found out that we could have a nurse come in and see to my mom, so that I don't have to miss school. Mr. Stanley over there gave me a job with less hours and more money, so that I have time to study. When it's slow at work, he says that I can get started on my homework. It's kind of bad to end up in D-Unit, but in a way, it's a good thing, too. It's going to help a lot of kids everybody else has given up on. Mr. Winters, I thank you for all that you've done and I promise — I'm going to college and I'm getting that degree in mechanical engineering."

The entire room exploded in applause.

Coco wiped away her tears.

Ransom hugged her. "You okay?"

"I'm so proud of them."

He nodded in agreement and then stood up. "Benjamin and Jerome, come over here, please."

They joined him.

Coco noted that they weren't wearing the really baggy pants this time. They'd dressed in shirts and ties, and jeans that were loose but didn't hang low. They both looked nice, she thought.

"You boys have committed yourselves to your education and I applaud your efforts. I also know that in order to accomplish the goals you've set for yourself you need tools. From all of us here at D-Unit, we would like to present you each with a set of encyclopedias. You'll also both get a laptop computer, donated by IBM."

The boys were speechless.

"We believe in you both and we know that you're capable of great things. From this moment forward, do not look to the things of the past. Keep your eyes on the horizon and face your future with pride."

Jerome hugged him. "Thank you, Mr. Winters. Thank you. I won't let you down."

Benjamin shook his hand. "I appreciate all you've done for me."

Coco walked over to Jerome. "I'm so proud of you."

He grinned. "I'm a lil' proud of myself."

"You should be," she told him. "In fact, you should be a lot proud."

She moved to Benjamin next. "I guess I'll be seeing you around a lot."

"You sure will."

"Please let me or Michael know if there's anything we can do for you and your family."

"Giving me this job was enough, Miss Stanley. I'm working twenty-five hours a week and I make twelve bucks an hour. I even have Sundays off now, so I can start going back to church."

"I'm so glad we could help. Benjamin, don't forget what I said. You are now a part of the Stanley Chocolates family."

"That's what your dad told me last night."

Coco was surprised. "You met my dad?"

"He came to the factory. He said that he liked to meet all the new hires."

Smiling, she nodded. "That's him. I don't know why I was so surprised earlier. He's been doing that ever since I can remember."

"Miss Stanley, you come from a real nice family. My mom's family was like that. Most of them are dead now, though."

"Do you have any family in this area?"

Benjamin shook his head. "My mom has one sister who lives in Texas. She's thinking about moving back to Los Angeles in case . . . in case my mom don't make it. She wants to be here for us."

"I'm going to keep her lifted in prayer."

"Thank you, Miss Stanley." He hugged her.

"Hey, let go of my woman," Ransom said.

"She a good one, Mr. Winters," Benjamin told him. "Don't do nothing stupid and lose her."

Ransom met her gaze and said, "Benjamin, I heard that."

"So I'm your woman now?" she asked in a low voice.

"Aren't you?" he countered.

Coco folded her arms across his shoulder. "Oh, no you don't. C'mon, spit it out."

"You're my woman," he told her, his eyes never leaving her face. "I don't want anyone else but you in my life."

She grinned. "That works for me. So, since I'm your woman, how about joining me tonight for dinner? I'll impress you with my cooking skills."

Yeah, right. Call the caterers.

"Sounds good," he responded. "I'm in the mood for a nice home-cooked meal."

Coco glanced at her watch. "I'd better get back to the shop or Valencia might up and quit on me."

Ransom walked her to the door. "Thanks for coming. I know that it meant a lot to Jerome and Benjamin. And me."

She stole a peek over her shoulder, to see the principal talking to the two teens. "I just hope he'll lift a hand to keep them on track."

"I'm meeting with him and the counselor after the boys leave."

Outside, Ransom kissed her. "See you tonight."

Coco had dinner ready by the time he arrived. She had prepared a simple meal of chicken alfredo over pasta, a garden salad and garlic bread.

She watched him as he took a bite. "How is it?"

"Delicious," he responded. "Why are you frowning? Is there something I don't know?"

"I'm just not known for my cooking in the kitchen. I'm great when it comes to mixing chocolate, but for stuff like this I have to follow a cookbook."

"That's because this is not your passion,"

Ransom said. "I love to cook. It's a passion of mine, just like music."

Marry me, please. Marry me and do all the cooking.

Ransom grinned as if he could hear her thoughts.

Coco felt a warm glow go through her, prompting her to take several sips of her iced tea. She couldn't keep from peering at him throughout dinner. She reveled in his nearness, her body aching for him in a way that she'd never felt for any other man.

Maybe it's time to pull out the dice and the chocolate body frosting.

Ransom was dealing with a battle of his own.

He felt heat radiating from his loins, and shifted in his seat, struggling to keep his desire for Coco under control. It had been much easier to maintain his vow of celibacy when he wasn't seeing anyone, but with a woman as beautiful, as fine as Coco, and the way her big brown eyes drew him in, it was a struggle.

Have mercy.

That's what his grandmother used to say. He'd never really understood why until now.

Ransom breathed a huge sigh of relief when Coco said, "I'm curious. Why do you care so much about these boys?" It forced his thoughts in another direction than the way they were going.

"I guess because I can relate," Ransom told her. "I didn't grow up with my father, and my mother worked all the time because she wanted to give me a good life. I was drawn to gangs because they gave me the family I was missing."

"You were part of a gang?" Coco asked.

"Not really," Ransom said. "I was drawn to them, but my mother and my grandmother weren't having it. My mom moved us in with Granny so that I wasn't home alone. My grandmother had no problem setting me straight whenever I needed a reminder."

Coco smiled. "Where *was* your father?"

"Around," Ransom said. "He wasn't with us — never was." He paused a moment before adding, "Coco, my father was married and had other children. He was separated when my mom met him, but he ended up going back to his wife."

"So you didn't get to spend any time with him?"

Ransom shook his head. "My father never knew about me."

"Would you like to meet him?"

"Yeah, it would've been nice, but I'll never

have that chance, sweetheart. He died a long time ago."

"What about your siblings?" Coco questioned. "Do they know anything?"

"They don't know that I exist," Ransom stated.

Coco met his gaze. "I hope I'm not bringing up any bad memories by having you talk about all this. I don't want to upset you."

"You're not," he replied. "I'm fine."

"Have you considered finding them?"

Ransom nodded. "I know where they are. It's just that my father's gone and I guess there's no point in upsetting them with this."

"I disagree. They are your family. Who knows, they may be very accepting of you, Ransom."

"And then again, they may not. I'm not willing to take that chance." Ransom swallowed his pain.

Coco wasn't buying his act, however. "I can tell that this is bothering you. I think you should contact your siblings."

"And tell them what? That their father had a relationship with my mother while he was still married to their mother?" Ransom shook his head. "I don't think so."

They settled down in the den after dinner.

"I've been meaning to ask you, just how many photo albums do you have?" Ransom pointed to the stack on the shelf beneath her coffee table.

"Lots," Coco responded with a chuckle. "I'm big on capturing memories. I carry a camera with me everywhere. The pictures on the wall — I took all those."

"Really? You're a very good photographer."

"I wanted my own studio at one time, but I'm a Stanley," she said. "Chocolate is what I do."

"Sweetheart, you do know that you can do both."

"You think so? You think I'm that good?"

Ransom nodded. "These pictures are excellent. Hey, can I hire you to be our official photographer for graduation ceremonies? You could do a much better job than I can."

"Are you serious?"

He nodded. "It would really help me out and I'll pay you."

"Ransom, you don't have to pay me. Consider it my gift to the boys. I'll even throw in sets for them."

He hugged her. "Now take me down memory lane. I want to see what you looked like as a high school student and then college."

"Why? Because you want a good laugh?"

"No, I'm just curious."

"Uh-huh," Coco uttered. "One chuckle and I'm booting you out of here."

Opening the blue-and-white album, she said, "This was my last year in high school. We lived in Riverside back then."

"Riverside?"

She nodded. "I graduated from Riverside High School. Did you go there?"

Ransom shook his head. "You were a cheerleader. Why am I not surprised?"

His eyes traveled to the girl standing next to her in the picture. He studied her face for a moment. A strange sensation stirred in him, prompting him to ask, "Who is she?"

Coco grinned. "Oh, that's my best friend, Elle. You know what? She has your first name for a last name."

He felt as if he had been kicked in the gut. "Her last name is R-Ransom?"

Coco nodded and turned the page, oblivious to the turbulent thoughts racing through his mind.

"This is when we went to the prom."

"Are these guys your dates?" he asked.

"Yeah," Coco answered. "This one was my date and Elle went with him." She pointed. "He turned out to be a jerk, though."

"What happened?"

"Oh, he got mad because she didn't want to sleep with him that night. Elle ended up riding home with me."

"It looks like you two were very close."

"We are. Our parents were best friends, so we spent a lot of time with them. Both of my brothers are close to Elle's brothers. In fact, Michael used to date Ivy. She's Elle's oldest sister. He was heartbroken when she married someone else."

Ransom was still reeling from the revelation that the woman he was dating shared a close relationship with his father's children. He didn't know exactly how many there were, and he wanted to ask, but knew that would stir Coco's curiosity.

He considered that he might have given her too much information on his past. What if she started putting two and two together?

No one knows about me.

His mother had often told him that he looked a lot like his father. If that were true, then wouldn't Coco have seen the similarities?

It angered him that she knew more about the other half of his family than he did. Coco showed him pictures from vacations that the two families had taken together. Ransom tried not to let it bother him, but it did.

"Hey, you okay?" she asked. She wore a look of concern on her face.

Ransom rose to his feet. "Actually, I'm not feeling well," he told her.

"Do you think my cooking made you sick?" Coco appeared alarmed. "The chicken was cooked all the way through. I —"

He cut her off by saying, "Sweetheart, it wasn't your cooking. Dinner was fine."

"But you're not feeling well. You were fine when you came over here."

"It's more from exhaustion," Ransom said. "Look, I know we were going to go out later for dessert, but I think I'm just going to go home. I've got a long day tomorrow. I'm sorry."

"Are you going to be able to drive?" she asked. "If you need me to, I can take you home. You can pick up your car tomorrow."

"I'll be fine."

Coco walked him to the door.

He kissed her goodbye, then left quickly.

Later at home, Ransom went through his own photo album.

"Why didn't you just tell him about me?" he whispered. "Why did you ever tell me about him? Didn't you know that I would try to seek him out?"

Ransom had a thought. "Maybe that's what you wanted me to do."

Something was wrong with Ransom.

He had been fine when he first arrived, so what could have upset him so much that he practically ran out of her house?

If it wasn't her chicken alfredo, then what happened to bring the evening to a sudden halt?

Coco replayed the events in her mind as she went back through the album, page by page.

She couldn't forget the pain she'd glimpsed in his eyes. She had never seen those beautiful, warm brown eyes look so sad.

Coco glanced at Elle's picture, and then frowned.

She picked up another album — the one with the Stanley-Ransom family vacation memories. Her eyes traveled to the pictures of Elle's brothers. Ray, Prescott and Laine looked most like their father, but even Ellie had their father's eyes.

She gasped.

"Oh, my goodness!" she uttered as she realized what Ransom must have seen. He had found his siblings. "Is this . . . could it be?"

What am I thinking? Ransom never saw his father.

But that didn't mean that he didn't have a photo of the man.

Coco decided to wait and see if Ransom said something to her. But until then, she was going to do some investigating on her own.

CHAPTER 8

The next day, Ransom surprised her at the shop with flowers and an apology. "I shouldn't have left like I did last night."

"Do you want to tell me what's going on with you?" she asked.

"I was tired," he told her. "It had nothing to do with your cooking."

"Are you sure?" she pressed. "Because you seemed more upset than anything."

Ransom couldn't quite read her expression, but felt that Coco knew more than she was letting on. "No, I was tired."

"Okay. Well, you don't owe me an apology," she said. "But the flowers were a really nice touch."

He smiled. "Can I make it up to you tonight?"

Coco gave a slight shrug. "Sure, if you're up to it."

"I am, because there's something I think that we need to discuss."

"This sounds really serious."

Ransom met her eyes. "It is, in my opinion, Coco."

"Okay," she said. "I'll see you tonight."

"I'll be there around seven."

"That's fine. Oh, you might want to bring dinner. I'm not cooking for you again until I'm sure the chicken wasn't the problem."

Ransom chuckled. "Coco, the chicken alfredo was great. I was just tired, and when I get that run-down, my body starts to crash. That's what happened."

There was that expression again.

Coco looked as if she expected some other reason. Had she figured out his secret? He didn't dare ask, in the event he was just being paranoid.

Could a relationship still work between them when she found out the truth? Coco was more family to the Ransoms than he was. If she had to pick a side, which would she choose?

Maybe it would be better to end things with her now. Ransom loved her and didn't want to put her in the middle of a mess that had been created by his mother.

Coco paced back and forth across the hardwood floor, her stomach full of nervous energy.

He's going to break up with me.

She could feel it.

It was torture waiting for Ransom to arrive. Coco wanted to get it over and done with.

The doorbell rang, startling her. She rushed to open the front door, then stepped aside so he could enter. He had stopped to pick up some dinner for them.

That's a good sign, right? He's not going to sit down and have dinner with me and then just dump me.

They didn't talk much while they ate.

Every now and then Coco would catch him staring at her. It was as if he were photographing her with his eyes.

That was a bad sign, she decided. In the past, they'd had stimulating conversations over meals. Coco couldn't take it anymore.

She pushed her plate away and said, "Ransom, what did you come here to talk about? I'd rather we get that out of the way."

"Coco, I'm going through something right now and . . . right now, I can't really talk about it because I have to figure some stuff out."

She wiped her mouth on the edge of her napkin before saying, "I thought as much."

"I came here with the intention of putting our relationship on hold until I could get some answers, but when I pulled into your driveway, I realized that I can't do it. I can't do it because I'm in love with you."

His gaze was riveted on her face. "I love you, Coco."

She opened her mouth to speak, but no words came out.

Did he just say the L word?

Coco tried again. "Please tell me that I didn't hear you wrong. Can you say it again, please?"

Ransom smiled. "I love you."

Impelled by her own emotions, Coco got up and walked around the table toward him.

He pushed his chair back and she sat down on his lap.

Gathering her into his arms, Ransom held her snugly. "This feels so right to me," he whispered. "I couldn't give you up."

"I love you, too, Ransom. I want you to know that you're not alone. We can get through anything you're facing — we can do it together."

I hope you're right, he thought silently.

She was watching him, studying his expression. Coco smiled then, stirring something within him.

"Sweetheart, there's something else that we need to talk about."

"What is it?"

"I'm celibate," Ransom blurted out. "I have been for five years."

"Oh . . . *Oh.*" Coco stood up and sat down in the chair beside him, trying not to laugh.

"As you can tell, my desire for you is in overdrive, but I can't act on it, sweetheart."

"I knew you were a Christian," she said.

"It's not just a label for me."

"You had to take it there, didn't you?" Coco asked.

He laughed.

"It's been a while for me, too," she said finally. "Not as long as you, but I am traveling down the same path. To be honest with you, my choice to remain abstinent had nothing to do with my faith, but more to do with my health. I enjoy living a disease-free life and I'd like to keep it that way."

They left the table and walked into the den.

Ransom pulled her into his arms, kissing her lips. His tongue sent shivers of desire racing through her. Coco matched him kiss for kiss.

Weakened by his yearning for her, Ransom pulled away, saying, "Sweetheart, we really have to stop."

"I know . . . but I don't want to," she moaned. The kiss had left her weak and a bit confused.

Ransom kissed the top of her head. "Coco, you have my flesh screaming for you right now."

It was going to take all of his willpower to walk out of her house tonight. Ransom was going to have to leave soon before he gave in to the passion that had been building ever since he first laid eyes on Coco.

CHAPTER 9

"I'm so glad you were able to meet me for lunch," Coco told Elle. "How have you been feeling lately?"

Two weeks had passed since her friends had found out she was pregnant.

"I'm still tired a lot, but it's not as bad as it was."

"I haven't talked to you since you had your doctor's appointment. How did it go?"

"Great," she answered. "I'm definitely pregnant. Almost twelve weeks, and Brennan is thrilled. We haven't told the boys yet. I want to wait until we're sure the pregnancy is viable."

"You had no idea?"

"Not at all," she responded.

"I'm so happy for you and Brennan."

Elle smiled. "We couldn't be more excited."

Coco scanned her menu, trying to decide what she wanted to eat.

The waiter came to take their order.

"How are your parents doing?" Elle asked after he left. "Mama told me she had lunch with your mom last week. I think they're getting together at least once or twice a month."

"My mom told me that they are going to start spending time at the spa. She said they're going to go at least once a week."

Elle raised her eyes in surprise. "Really? I think that's great. I've been trying to get Mama to do something like that for years. I wonder why she's suddenly decided to follow my advice."

"She's probably doing it because my mom is going with her," Coco said. "Maybe she didn't want to go alone."

"I would've gone with her," Elle stated.

"It's not the same as when you and I go to the spa. It's different when Mama and I go."

The food arrived.

Elle said grace. Then, picking up her fork, she murmured, "I guess you're right. What are Aunt Eleanora and Uncle Daniel up to?"

"They're getting ready to take a cruise to Greece," Coco announced. "My mother's been wanting to visit there for a long time now. They have been traveling more since Dad retired."

"Is Michael running the business?" Elle asked. "Mama said your dad retired a few months ago."

"Mama made him do it," Coco said with a short laugh. "Daddy went kicking and screaming. Michael manages the factory and Daniel is overseeing the stores."

"My father loved working for the company."

"Daddy says that he was the best accountant they'd ever had. We all still think about your father a lot," she told Elle. "He was a really nice man."

"I don't really remember him like the others do, but I still miss him."

"I can't imagine what I'd do if something happened to my dad."

"You'd find a way to go on," Elle said. "You hold on to the memories that you shared. Nothing can take them away from you. At least that's what my mother always says."

"I always thought that your parents had the perfect marriage," Coco told her. "I feel the same way about my parent's marriage."

Elle shook her head. "Trust me, Coco. No marriage is perfect. When Brennan and I were dealing with the baby mama drama, my mom told me that she and my dad separated at one point, but they found their way back to each other. Marriage is hard work, but when you truly love each other you can work through anything."

"Do you and Brennan ever see Lauren?"

"Not really," Elle responded between bites. "When he found out that she wasn't his child, but his sister, it messed him up. He loves Lauren, but he still hasn't forgiven Charis for the deception. I think he feels betrayed mostly by his father. That's what bothers him the most."

"You handled it well when you thought that Lauren was your stepdaughter." Coco sliced off a piece of her stuffed flounder and stuck it in her mouth.

Elle shrugged. "There was nothing else I could do. It wasn't her fault — she didn't ask to come into this world. I couldn't stand Charis, though." She took a sip of her water. "Coco, I'll be honest with you. It did bother me when I thought another woman had my husband's child. It would bother any woman."

Coco didn't respond.

After lunch, she went back to the shop and stayed until her assistant manager arrived.

"I'm leaving early today," Coco told Valencia. "Bryan will be in around two thirty. He's working until closing."

She left and drove over to her parents' house.

Maybe I can get some answers from my dad. He and Uncle Prescott were close friends, so they probably confided in one another.

Coco found her father out in the backyard. One of his favorite pastimes was gardening.

"Hey, Daddy."

"I'm a little surprised to see you, Coco. I thought you'd be creating another one of your delicacies."

"I meant to bring you some of my chocolate-covered oranges," she told him. "They're delicious."

He gave her a sidelong glance. "Chocolate doesn't go with everything, sweetheart."

"But it does, Daddy," she said with a smile. "You just have to find the right ingredients."

Coco followed him into his office.

"So what did you come here to discuss, baby?"

She sat down on the love seat beside him, her fingers tense in her lap. As casually as she could manage, she asked, "Daddy, do you remember anything about the time Aunt Amanda and Uncle Prescott were separated?"

"Honey, that was a long time ago and it has nothing to do with you."

Awkwardly, she cleared her throat. "Daddy, I think there's something you should know."

His body seemed to tense up. "What is it, sweetheart?"

"I think Ransom might be Uncle Prescott's son."

Her father's expression remained blank. "Why do you say that?"

"Lots of reasons," Coco replied. "For one thing, his name is Ransom, and he looks a lot like them. I didn't realize it until we were going through the photo albums."

"We? Ransom was with you?" her father asked.

Coco nodded.

"How did he respond?"

"We didn't talk about it, Daddy. I'm not sure he's figured it out yet, but he will eventually. All he knows is that his father was separated when he got involved with Ransom's mother, and then he decided he wanted to be with his wife and kids, so he broke off the relationship, not knowing that she was carrying his child."

Coco eyed her father. He didn't seem too surprised by what she was telling him. "You already knew this, didn't you?"

"I suspected it when I met him," he admitted. "Prescott told me about the woman. Her name was Robina Winters. He cared for her, but it was Amanda he loved. When your young man told me his name was Ransom Winters, I knew."

"So what do we do?" Coco asked.

"Nothing," her father stated. "If Ransom is seeking answers, let him be the one to find them. You don't need to stir up trouble — it will find its way all on its own. Trust me on that."

"Are you telling me that I shouldn't tell Ransom that my best friend is his sister?"

"Coco, you don't say a word. If he's looking for them, he will find them. You stay out of this, because it could all blow up in your face."

She only half listened as she struggled with her conscience. Coco felt as if she was betraying all of them by withholding this information. She knew that Elle would want to know if she had another brother walking around somewhere. Coco knew that Ransom wanted to meet his siblings.

"Sweetheart, I hope you're listening to me," her father said.

She couldn't help frowning in response. "I heard you, Daddy. I just wish I didn't know any of this. I hate being in the middle of this situation."

"Then take yourself out of it," her father

advised. "And Coco, *stay* out of it. It's best all around."

She stirred uneasily in her chair, hoping against hope that her father was right.

"Okay, to make dark chocolate, you need chocolate liquor, sugar and vanilla," Coco announced as she and Ransom walked through the factory. She had come over to check on an order that was about to be shipped.

Ransom had tagged along with her so that he could check on Benjamin. He and Coco were deep into a conversation on the chocolate-making process.

"The ingredients are mixed together and kneaded until well blended," she explained.

"You're so comfortable in this environment, but you panic in the kitchen," Ransom noted.

"I spent a big part of my life in this factory, but not much time in the kitchen preparing meals," Coco responded.

"You really are a good cook. You just don't give yourself enough credit."

She hugged him. "That's my baby."

"So is this the same way you make milk chocolate?" Ransom asked.

"You know what? I'm going to let Benjamin answer that for you."

"Mr. Winters, it's like this. To make milk chocolate, the milk and sugar are mixed together and then blended with chocolate liquor."

"So what is your job?" Ransom asked.

"After everything is mixed, it comes through this machine right here," he said, pointing to a series of heavy rollers. "I make sure that the mixture travels through here smoothly. It can take up to seven days to finish this process."

Ransom seemed impressed.

"Do you remember what this process is called?" Coco asked Benjamin.

"Conching," he answered with a smile.

"You're doing a great job," she told him.

"My grades are up, too," he said. "I passed all of my final exams. I'm glad school is almost out because I'm going to work forty hours during the summer." Benjamin smiled. "I'll be able to get all of us some school clothes for next year."

"Benjamin, I don't want you worrying about college," Ransom said. "If you get accepted, I will pay for your tuition and books."

"You serious?"

He nodded. "You have to do your part, though."

"I will. I wasn't going to take the SAT

because I didn't think I'd be able to save enough money for college."

"Stanley Chocolates also gives scholarships," Coco announced.

"I can get one because I work here?"

She nodded. "You sure can. Like Ransom just said, bring in your college acceptance letter and we'll start the paperwork."

Benjamin looked upward. "Thank you, God," he whispered.

Coco walked away to keep from crying.

One of the older men who worked in the factory came over. "He's a good kid," he told her. "And a hard worker. I'm glad y'all took a chance on this one."

"Thank you, Sam."

She headed back to her shop. It was almost time for Valencia to clock out, and Coco was working until closing tonight.

Ransom rejoined her a few minutes later.

"I'm going to have to stay on him about that SAT. He needs to go on and get it out of the way."

Ransom's going to make a great father one day.

Coco felt a thread of guilt over the secret she was keeping from him. He deserved to know, but she couldn't risk tearing apart Elle's family.

Ransom gave her a slight nudge. "Hey, I

113

thought you were telling me about the chocolate-making process. So what comes after the kneading?"

Coco smiled. "Tempering," she responded. "This process allows you to solidify chocolate. After that the mixture is poured into molds and placed in a cooling chamber."

"This is just the base for you, though," Ransom said. "You add more ingredients for your gourmet products, right?"

"Yes. I add spices, flavors, fruit — whatever it calls for."

"So if I give you some ingredients, do you think you could create a candy bar with them?"

Coco met his gaze. "Is this a challenge?"

Ransom nodded.

She spoke eagerly. "What do I get if I win?"

"What do you want?"

She broke into a smile.

Before she said anything, Ransom cocked his head to the side and said, "I'm going to regret this, aren't I?"

"It won't be so bad. If I win, I want you to take violin lessons for two weeks."

"That's it?" he asked. When she nodded, Ransom held out his hand. "Okay, you're on."

She shook hands with him. "Okay, give me the ingredients."

"I only have one," he said. "Applewood bacon."

"Excuse me? You want me to come up with a bacon bar?"

Ransom nodded. "You can use any other ingredients you like, but it has to have bacon."

Bacon. I'm not real sure about this, but there is no way I'm going to let Ransom win this challenge.

"Are you certain? You want bacon in chocolate?"

He nodded a second time. "What doesn't go with bacon?"

"Chocolate," Coco responded. "I'm up to the challenge, but I'm not sure on this one, Ransom."

"Give it your best shot, sweetheart."

"You can count on that," Coco said. "I'm not about to let you win."

Ransom laughed. "We'll see."

He showed no signs of relenting.

"Okay," Coco said. "I'll get started on it tomorrow. This is going to be so much fun. I'm going to enjoy teaching you the fundamentals of playing the violin."

"We'll see," he repeated. Then he raked his eyes boldly over her body.

Coco found herself extremely conscious of Ransom's virile appeal. She yearned to be crushed in his embrace, and ached for his touch. Her feelings for him were intensifying.

Before either one of them said a word, they fell into each other's arms, kissing hungrily.

The sound of the door opening forced them apart.

"I'll see you later, Ransom."

She didn't dare look up at the person standing in the doorway for fear he knew why her face was so flushed.

On Saturday, a frustrated Coco spent the day in the factory kitchen. "Michael, I have to win this challenge," she said. "But I'm not really getting anywhere."

"What have you tried so far?" he asked.

"Just about everything," Coco admitted. "I keep thinking about chocolate chip pancakes, bacon and syrup. It's the perfect combination, but my challenge is incorporating that in chocolate."

She pointed to a mixing bowl. "I tried combining the chocolate, syrup and bacon in there, but the bacon was too salty."

"You've been at this all morning," Michael told her. "Why don't you take a break?"

"What about the salt from alder wood smoke? Michael, do you have any over here?"

"I'll get it for you," he said. "But why are you doing all this? For Ransom? Why is it so important?"

"Because you know how competitive I am," Coco answered. "Michael, you know that I have to win."

"I don't know about this one, sis. Candy with pieces of applewood bacon in it?"

She nodded. "I have to keep trying."

She mixed wood-smoked salt into the milk chocolate and bacon combination. "Since it's bacon, I'm thinking this will do the trick."

Michael didn't look convinced.

"Try it," she said.

"I tried the last couple of batches," he told her. "I have to sing tomorrow at church. You're not going to make me ill."

"Chicken," she muttered, and sampled the mixture. "Michael, you've got to try it. I like it."

He shook his head.

"Please . . ."

Michael dipped a spoon into the mixture, then another. "This is good." He gave her a thumbs-up.

"I hope Ransom's ready for violin lessons," she said, pouring the batch into the molds.

I win. I win.

CHAPTER 10

Coco pulled the folds of her sweater together as she and Ransom strolled along the beach. She could hardly wait for them to get back to his house so that she could give him the candy bar. She had even designed a custom label that read D-Unit's Bacon Bar.

"Cold?"

"It's a little breezy out here, but I'm fine," she told him. "I love being out here on the beach. I can see why you bought a house in Santa Monica. It's beautiful out here at night."

Ransom agreed. "I like coming out here in the evenings. Not a lot of people."

She looked up at him. "You come down here often?"

"In the evenings?" he asked.

When she nodded, he replied, "Not as much as I'd like."

"I love it out here. It's very romantic,"

Coco said. "You know . . . moonlit walks and all."

"So you consider this romantic?" Ransom teased. "Our walking on the beach in the moonlight."

Coco gave him a playful slap on the arm. "Yeah, I do." She savored the sultry sounds of Ransom's laughter. The man was sexy through and through. . . .

"What are you thinking about?" he asked.

"You and how you make me feel." She rubbed her arms through the sweater, trying to ward off the goose bumps from the brisk ocean air.

"I don't make you itch, do I?"

Laughing, she shook her head. "Not at all."

Ransom wrapped an arm around her. "Better?"

Nodding, Coco replied, "Much better."

After their walk along the sandy shoreline, she and Ransom sat down on a huge beach towel that he'd pulled out the trunk of his car, talking as they watched the waves splash toward them and retreat.

"What would you like to talk about now?" Coco asked.

"How about this?" Ransom leaned forward and kissed her.

His kiss was slow and thoughtful, and sent

spirals of desire racing through her. "Mmm . . . I love the subject matter."

"Why don't we head back to the house?" Ransom suggested. "I know that you're cold."

"Thank you," she said with a chuckle.

They left the beach and went to his house.

Coco loved the design of Ransom's home and the amazing ocean, mountain and city-lights views from the many rooms. He had given her a tour the first time she came to the five-bedroom house with its fabulous West Indies decor throughout.

From where she was standing now, she had a fantastic view of the outdoor-lit, colorful flower garden, the raging ocean and the sprawling deck out back. Ransom was having an outdoor kitchen installed. Grilling was one of his favorite pastimes.

Coco turned away from the window.

This area is so beautiful, she thought. Her eyes traveled from the faux-finished stucco walls to the hand-painted furniture to the huge overstuffed sofas. She'd asked him why he had so many bedrooms, and Ransom responded that they came with the house. Then he'd told her that he wanted to marry and settle down, so he'd kept that in mind while searching for a home.

She glanced down at the marble floor.

Coco loved hardwoods, but she had to admit Ransom's flooring was really nice.

"So, remember that little challenge you issued to me?" she asked.

He grinned. "You want to back out?"

She shook her head. "Not at all, baby."

"Then what?"

Coco pulled a candy bar out of her purse. "I've been waiting all night to give this to you."

Ransom read the label and laughed. "D-Unit's Bacon Bar. I like the name."

"Taste it," she said. "I want to see what you think."

He opened it and took a bite.

Coco held her breath. She and Michael thought the candy tasted pretty good. But she figured Ransom's vote would be the one that counted.

"I'm impressed," he said after a moment. "I really didn't think you'd be able to come up with anything that tasted good. This is excellent."

"Are you serious? Do you really like it?"

"Yeah," Ransom answered. "I think you should consider adding it to your product line. You might want to change the name, though."

"I love the name, and now that you've said that, it sounds like a great idea. We could sell it, and all the proceeds will go to your center. We'll use it as a fund-raiser. I think we need to come up with a couple more, since not everyone eats bacon."

Ransom scanned her face. "You're really serious about this?"

She nodded. "It's really a good idea."

"You are a sweetheart," he told her. "I'm touched by your gesture and your generosity."

Coco placed her hand in his. "I thought we were a team, Ransom. You are always saying that it takes a village — well, I'm part of that village."

"This is one of the reasons why I love you."

She placed her arms around his neck. "I love you, too."

"Even with chocolate on my breath?"

"Yeah, but go brush your teeth."

Coco made herself comfortable on the sofa while Ransom went up to his bedroom.

Things were going well between them.

She was glad that she hadn't gone running her mouth to Ransom about his siblings. He never said anything, so apparently he didn't know that they were only a connection away.

Her father was right. This was the best way for everyone concerned. None of them deserved to be hurt by the past.

She did it.

Ransom broke into a grin. Coco had actually made a candy bar with bits of applewood bacon.

He went back downstairs and found her curled on the sofa.

She looked up when he entered the room. "What took you so long?"

"I wasn't gone that long, was I?"

Coco sat up to make room for him.

"Did you pick out something to watch? Most of the movies might be in the media room," he said.

"This movie is on TV," she announced. "It looks pretty interesting."

Ransom's thoughts began to wander when the movie didn't capture his interest.

Coco seemed into it, so he didn't complain.

He wanted to ask her more questions about the Ransom family, but didn't want to rouse her suspicions. Ransom hated the yearning inside him — the yearning to get to know his siblings. Things were complicated by the fact that his father was dead. There were DNA tests that could prove his claim, but he didn't want to cast a shadow on the image they had of Prescott Randolph

Ransom.

"Don't forget you have to take violin lessons for two weeks," Coco said during a TV commercial.

"I haven't forgotten," he told her. "I'm a man of my word."

She looked over at him. "Ransom, I know that much about you."

He reached up and stroked her cheek. "What else do you know about me?"

For a brief moment, she looked startled by his question. "That you are a man with a heart for teens. You're very handsome — not to mention extremely sexy. You're the man that I love."

Ransom pulled her into his arms, holding her close to him as if she were his lifeline.

She must have sensed his momentary desperation, because she lifted her head, studying his face. "What's wrong?"

He pasted on a smile. "Nothing."

"Ransom, I'm not sure I believe you," she responded. "You can tell me anything, you know?"

"Everything is fine, sweetheart," he said, trying to reassure her. "I am with the woman I love, so everything is right in my world."

The only thing missing is family, he added silently.

CHAPTER 11

It was time for Ransom to pay up.

Coco handed him his instrument. "This is what you'll be using for the next two weeks," she told him.

"You don't really expect me to learn to play this thing in just two weeks, do you?"

"No, but you will be able to play a simple song when I'm done," she responded. "The first thing you should know is that violins don't have frets like those found on guitars."

"I knew that," he said. "I think the issue for me is going to be positioning this thing on my neck. It looks uncomfortable."

"It takes getting used to," Coco admitted.

Ransom sat down and followed her instructions.

"There are four positions on the violin," she told him. "The first position is the farthest away from your face and produces low-pitched notes. The fourth position produces the highest notes."

He smiled at her. "I have a new respect for your gift. I'll be doing well if I'm able to tell you about the strings, sweetheart."

"You'll be fine," Coco assured him. "Just trust me."

Not much was accomplished during his first session, which didn't bother Ransom at all. He was not looking to be a violinist — he was just paying off a gambling debt. He'd lost what he thought would've been a surefire win.

Actually, it was turning out not to be such a bad loss. Coco was going to carry the new chocolate bar in her store, with the proceeds going to the center.

Later, at home, he sat down at the table and wrote the lyrics to a new song. He had gone for almost four months without writing. He blamed it on the move to the new house and getting the center ready.

But today he had been inspired by Coco.

He went over the lyrics once more before calling it a night. Ransom had an early morning parent meeting.

He was tired, but he wasn't sleepy.

Coco infiltrated his thoughts, taking over.

A smile tugged at his lips as he recalled how excited she'd been over winning their bet. Ransom hadn't realized how competitive she was until recently. He was learning more and more about her every day.

It didn't change his feelings for her. In fact, it only made him love her more, if that was possible.

Ransom felt a sense of accomplishment by the end of the two weeks.

He could play "Mary Had a Little Lamb." He had learned a lot about the instrument, how the strings were tuned and how to change the tone by applying more pressure.

He was in his office going over paperwork that needed to be sent to the schools when one of the staff came to the door announcing that Ransom had a visitor.

He walked out, expecting to see Coco, but instead found his old writing partner, Jaye, standing there.

"What's up?" he said.

"I heard you were doing your thing over here, and since I was in the area, I thought I'd drop by."

"It's good to see you, man." Ransom gestured for him to enter his office and take a seat. "Jaye, what have you been up to?"

"I'm producing this new artist — Ransom, you need to hear her. I'm telling you, she's gonna blow this town apart. Not just L.A., but the whole country."

"She must be something if you're this

excited about her."

"Ransom, the girl was born to do this. Anyway, in my agreement with the record company, they're guaranteeing that I get to write four of the songs on the record. I know you're really focused on the center right now, but I need you, man. I know if we do this together, those cuts are gonna be the cream of the crop."

Ransom smiled. "You always say that."

"And I'm always right, too."

"Let me think about it, Jaye."

"Ransom, school's almost out, so it's not like you'll have the center open."

"Actually, I'll be keeping it open through the summer. We plan to offer tutoring sessions and SAT preparation classes along with some other subjects."

"You and I — we can do this, man."

Ransom considered the offer as Jaye outlined all of the details. They worked well together and their collaborations had won numerous awards. He wanted to open more centers and the extra money could be put aside for that.

It would mean not spending as much time with Coco, but he was pretty sure she'd understand.

"So what do you say?" Jaye prompted.

"I'll do it," Ransom answered.

They shook hands.

When Jaye left, Ransom walked over to see Coco.

She was assisting a customer when he arrived. Ransom took a seat at the bar and waited for her to finish.

"What are you doing over here?" she asked. "I thought you were going to the high school this afternoon."

"I am," he told her. "But I wanted to talk to you about something."

"What is it?"

"A friend of mine came to see me not too long ago. He and I have collaborated on a lot of songs."

"Does he want you to work on a project?" Coco asked.

"Actually, four of them," Ransom responded. "I accepted the offer only so that I could invest the money in the centers. We get some funding from the government, but it's not enough for what I have in mind."

"It's a great opportunity for you," Coco told him.

"But it means we won't be spending as much time together as planned," Ransom said. "I just want to make sure you know what to expect. I don't want you to start thinking that I don't want to be with you or anything like that."

"I understand, Ransom."

"Are you okay with it?"

She nodded. "We'll still have some time together, right?"

"Yeah, of course. I'm not going to walk out of your life. It's just that I have to make time for my writing — something I haven't done in a while."

"Then you need to make time to do that," Coco said. "Your writing is your income. I totally understand that. Besides, I've got the Chocolate Expo this summer and the Candy Expo."

Ransom checked the clock on the wall and said, "I need to get going. I have to go check on my boys. We can talk more about this when I get back."

"Tell Jerome that I said hello."

He kissed her.

Ransom left the shop feeling pretty good about his life. He didn't really have any family left, but he was with the woman he loved, and the structured day program was doing well. Now he had a chance to earn monies for the program. Life was good.

Coco almost dropped the mug she was holding when Elle, Kaitlin and their sister-in-law, Carrie, walked through the front door. Ransom had just left, so she wondered if they had run into him outside.

She scanned their faces to see if she could detect anything.

"What's wrong with you?" Kaitlin asked. "You look like you've seen a ghost."

Coco pasted on a smile. "I'm sorry. I was just startled for a moment."

They sat down at the bar.

"What are you three doing?" Coco asked, trying to sound normal. "Retail therapy?"

Elle laughed. "Actually, we just had lunch and thought we'd come say hello to you. Where have you been? I haven't heard from you in a while. I guess you and Ransom are getting along well."

"Ransom?" Carrie asked.

"She's dating a guy named Ransom. Isn't that wild?"

Carrie nodded. "Is that his first name?"

"Yeah. He owns D-Unit across the street."

"Things have been crazy here at the shop," Coco told Elle. "But Ransom and I are doing well."

"I figured as much," she replied.

"Elle, how are you feeling?" Coco inquired, before her friend started asking when or if they were going to meet him. That was not a question she wanted to answer.

"Great. The baby and I are doing fine."

Coco smiled. "That's good to hear."

"I need to get some more of that body frosting," Kaitlin said with a grin.

"I can't keep this stuff in stock. If it's really as much fun as you all say, then I can't wait to get married," Coco exclaimed. "I'm going to have to stash a few cans for me. Everybody comes in here raving about it."

"It's wonderful, girl," Kaitlin said. "It's so wonderful that I think I might be pregnant. I'm late and that almost never happens."

Elle squealed with delight.

"When are you going to take a test?" Coco asked.

"I'm going to wait until the end of next week. I want to make sure my cycle's not just late coming this month."

"You'd know right away with a pregnancy test," Elle told her. "You don't have to wait."

"I know, but I don't mind waiting. Oh, who am I trying to kid? I'm dying to know."

"Then go get a pregnancy test. You can take it right here in the shop," Elle said.

Coco and Carrie agreed.

Kaitlin left to walk down to the grocery store to purchase a test.

"I hope she's pregnant," Elle said. "I want our babies to grow up together."

Carrie went to the bathroom in the back,

and a moment later a customer entered the shop.

Valencia waited on her while Coco poured a glass of ice water for Elle. She set the bottle down beside the glass.

"Is this your way of saying I need to drink more water?" Elle asked.

"I'm just leaving it here in case you want more, that's all." Coco knew how much her friend hated drinking water.

Carrie returned and reclaimed her seat.

"Just remember that when you're pregnant, I'm going to police you. I know you hate taking pills, but you're going to have to get used to the prenatal vitamins. In fact, you should start them before you plan to get pregnant."

Coco shuddered at the thought of taking any kind of pills. She hated them. "Elle, that's wrong on so many levels."

"So is making me drink all this water."

She laughed. "Elle, I'm not making you do anything. If you're feeling conflicted it's not because of me."

Kaitlin returned with a small bag. "Got it."

They waited while she took the test.

A couple of minutes later, she walked back out with a big smile on her face. "Matt is going to be thrilled," Kaitlin said. "I'm pregnant."

Coco gave her a hug and then Carrie.

Kaitlin and Elle embraced.

Several customers came into the shop.

"I'll be back," Coco said to her friends. "I need to help Valencia on the sales floor."

She walked with a customer over to the bar. "Which one of the dessert toppings would you like?"

"I'll take two bottles of the strawberry champagne," the woman decided. "I'd also like some white-chocolate-covered peanuts. I need a quarter . . . no, make that a half pound of them. A quarter pound of the orange crème and white chocolate bars."

Coco rang up her order. "It comes to sixty-four dollars and twenty cents."

Kaitlin stole a peek over her shoulder. "Looks like she's preparing for a chocoholic party."

Ransom burst through the door. "Hey —"

He stopped abruptly when his eyes landed on Elle and Kaitlin.

Composing himself, Ransom said, "I — I'll give you a call later."

All Coco could do was nod.

She was pretty sure that he'd seen the truth in her eyes.

Coco knew the truth.

That was the only reason she would stand there and look so guilty.

A thought occurred to him. Had she already said anything to them?

Ransom was blown away by the mere possibility that Coco had somehow figured out the truth, but never mentioned it.

But how long had she known? That question plagued him.

And why didn't she ever say anything to him? Had she put it all together because he'd opened his big mouth? He never should have told her about his father's family.

Ransom prayed she hadn't said anything to them — he didn't want to cause trouble for that family. He was tempted to call Coco and tell her to keep her mouth shut regarding his parentage, but felt that would look suspicious, so he aborted the idea.

Maybe I'm overreacting, he told himself silently. *All this stuff about my absent father and wanting to meet my siblings has made me a little crazy.*

All Ransom wanted to do now was stay as far away from them as possible. He couldn't bear the thought of bringing an ounce of hurt to that family. He had been selfish in his desire to get to know them.

Ransom decided to abort the idea.

The price was just too high.

"Okay, who was that?" Kaitlin asked, recovering from her shock.

"For a second, I thought it was Laine," Carrie said.

"Whoever he was, he looked like he could be a member of this family. He looked like a Ransom," Elle contributed.

Carrie said what no one else was willing to ask. "I know everybody is supposed to have a twin, but is it possible that you have another brother or cousin you don't know about?" She was partly joking.

"It's always possible to have a cousin we haven't met," Kaitlin said with a chuckle.

"You know Uncle Jules used to be a big-time playa."

There was no getting around it this time. Coco swallowed hard before saying, "His name is Ransom Winters."

The room grew silent.

"That was Ransom?" Elle asked. "The guy you've been dating all this time?"

"He really could be Uncle Jules's son," Kaitlin responded. "This is so weird."

Coco silently debated whether or not to tell them what Ransom had shared with her. The uncle they were talking about had lost his wife in childbirth almost thirty years ago and didn't remarry until ten or eleven years after that.

I should just keep quiet. But how can I? Coco cleared her throat nervously.

"What do you know?" Elle asked. "You always do that when you're feeling anxious over something."

Elle knew her too well.

"If you know something, tell us," Kaitlin pleaded.

"His father was separated from his wife when he met Ransom's mother," Coco told them. "He later went back to his wife, but he didn't know that he was about to be a father. She never told him. She named him Ransom because she wanted him to have some part of his father."

"Did Ransom tell you all that?" Kaitlin asked.

Coco nodded.

"Does he know who his father was?" Elle wanted to know.

"Yes, he does," Coco replied.

"Is it Uncle Jules?" Elle asked quietly.

Coco shook her head sadly. She could see the pain etched on her friend's face. Elle already suspected the truth, but wasn't ready to face it. "I'm pretty sure that it's your father."

"Does he know about us?" Kaitlin asked. "Is that why he ran out of here like a bat out of hell?"

Coco met Kaitlin's gaze. "He does know that there are other children. Ransom knows he has siblings. We were going through my high school photo albums and he saw pictures of you. I mentioned that you were a Ransom and I guess that's when things clicked for him."

"The way he left here . . . It's pretty obvious that he doesn't want to get to know us," Elle said.

"It's not that," Coco said. "Elle, I think he's afraid of being rejected, and he doesn't want to cause your mother any trauma."

Kaitlin rose to her feet. "Do you know where he went? I'd really like to talk to him."

"So would I," Elle said. "We all need some answers, I'm sure."

Coco nodded. "He's most likely in his office across the street. Ransom is the owner of D-Unit."

Elle looked surprised. "That's right. You did tell us that he had the same name, but it didn't register that we could possibly be related."

"You mean the music store over there?" Carrie questioned.

"Actually, it's not a music store," Coco explained. "It's a center for teens — a structured day program."

Carrie grabbed her purse. "I say we head over there and get to know this Ransom."

"I'll go with you," Coco said. She wasn't about to let Ransom face this alone. "I just need to wait until Bryan gets here to help Valencia."

"Coco, why didn't you tell us any of this before?" Elle asked plaintively.

"I wasn't a hundred percent sure and I didn't want to upset you, especially while you're pregnant."

Bryan arrived for work five minutes later.

Coco escorted the women across the street and into the center. Ransom was in his office. She knocked on the door.

He glanced up from his desk. "Coco —"

"They wanted to talk to you," she said lamely. "This is Kaitlin, Elle and Carrie Ransom."

He sent her a sharp glare, then gave the other women a tight smile. "Hello, ladies. Please come in."

They settled on the sofa while Coco walked around the desk to stand beside Ransom.

140

Kaitlin spoke first. "I'm sure you have an idea of why we came here to see you. It appears that you might be related to us."

Ransom did not respond. He gazed at Coco, who was becoming increasingly uncomfortable. She wanted to be anywhere but here, but would not abandon the man she loved.

"Can you tell us about your mother and how she came to meet our dad?" Elle inquired. "You were told that Prescott Ransom was your father, right?"

"My mother's name is Robina Winters and she met your father in Corona, where she lived. He and your mother were separated at the time. My mom said that he was still very much in love with your mom, so she decided it was best that they end their relationship. Your father went back home, and shortly after that my mom discovered she was pregnant. She didn't tell him."

Elle studied his face. "I'm sorry for staring at you like this, but you look like my brother Laine."

Kaitlin and Carrie agreed.

"Wait a minute! I know who you are," Elle blurted. "I knew that your name sounded familiar. You're a songwriter. You worked on some projects for Jupiter Records."

He smiled. "I'm surprised you know that."

"I work for Jupiter as a publicist."

"Ransom, would you be willing to take a DNA test?" Kaitlin asked hesitantly.

"Sure," he responded. "Look, if I had my way, you wouldn't know anything about me. I'm not looking for anything from your family."

"That's not why I was asking," Kaitlin replied quickly. "I believe you are who you say you are, but I just thought it would leave no room for assumptions. Our other brothers and sisters may desire something more definitive."

Coco offered a tiny smile, but Ransom's expression didn't change. She could tell that he was furious with her. She was having trouble understanding why. Especially since finding his siblings was what he wanted most in life. He wanted a family.

"This is awkward," Kaitlin said. "All this time, there has been another Ransom walking around and we had no clue." She took a deep breath. "Ransom, I'd like for you to come to Riverside on Sunday, so that you can meet the whole family."

He gave her a polite smile. "Thank you, Kaitlin. It's a nice offer, but I'm not sure I should accept it. This is a lot to take in and the rest of your family has no idea that I exist. I think it's best if all of you took some

142

time to digest everything. That goes for me, too."

She met his gaze straight on. "If you won't come to us, then we'll have no choice but to come to you. I need you to understand something — what it means to be a Ransom. We are a family, and if you're one of us, that makes you family, too. Everyone needs to meet you."

"I'm not sure they will be as accepting as you and Elle seem to be," Ransom said. "This is a lot to deal with."

"We're strong enough to handle anything that comes our way," she responded. "There was a time I couldn't have stood here and said something like that, but after everything I've been through, this is a piece of cake."

Ransom looked puzzled.

"At one point my family thought I'd died in a plane crash," Kaitlin explained. "Instead, I was basically held prisoner in Mexico. I pretended to have amnesia, and married my captor to stay alive."

He was shocked.

"We all have stories to tell," Carrie said. "Including you."

"Mine doesn't come close to what you must have experienced," he told Kaitlin. "How did you escape?"

"Matt St. Charles, he's my husband now,

143

and some of his friends came looking for me. I'll tell you the whole story one day." She smiled. "If you'll let me."

"I'd like to hear it."

"Ransom, please consider coming on Sunday," Elle pleaded. "You have nieces and nephews, brothers and sisters that I know will want to meet you. And my mother — she'll definitely want to meet you, too."

"Maybe you should check with them first," Ransom suggested. "It might be a good idea to have the DNA test, too."

She shook her head. "I don't need a test to prove what I already know. Kaitlin's right. If you won't come, then we're going to come looking for you. Carrie's husband and . . . our brother Ray . . . is a U.S. Marshal, and he'll find you. Matt . . . well, he was in special ops, so he can find you, too."

Laughing, Ransom gazed at Coco, who nodded and said, "I'll go with you if you want me to."

He didn't respond.

Carrie looked from one to the other. "Please don't be mad with Coco. This is not her fault. When we saw you, we knew something was up. You look too much like members of this family, and then you carry the name Ransom . . . We put this together."

His silence stung for some reason. This had to be a weird situation for him, Coco told herself, and he didn't need to deal with her insecurities right now.

"We have to get going," Elle said. "Ransom, I hope you will come to Riverside on Sunday. We need to talk this through — all of us."

"I'll give it some serious thought, but that's all I can promise at this point. I'm sorry."

She nodded.

"We'll talk later," Coco said to him.

Ransom's eyes never left her face. "Definitely."

CHAPTER 12

"I don't need a DNA test to tell me that Ransom is my brother," Elle stated. "I can feel it in my heart — he's one of us."

"I have to say I'm with you on that," Kaitlin said.

"What do you think your brothers and sisters will say?" Carrie asked. "I'm not sure Ray is going to handle this well. You know how much he adored his father."

"I don't think any less of my dad," Elle responded. "It's not like he cheated on Mama. They were separated."

"They were still married," Kaitlin interjected. "How do you think Mama is going to feel? This is my biggest concern — what it will do to her. Elle, you've been there. You know what it feels like."

"That was just some drama, though. It's not quite the same. Besides, Daddy is gone and we're all grown. Personally, I think she'll handle it like she's handled everything else."

Carrie and Kaitlin agreed.

"I'm pretty sure that Ray is going to insist on a DNA test," Carrie stated. "Laine and Prescott probably will also."

"I'm really sorry for not coming to you with this before now," Coco said. "I had my suspicions about Ransom, but I didn't know how to tell you. It's not like I had any real proof, and I didn't want to just jump to conclusions."

Elle nodded in understanding. "I guess I would feel the same way if I were in your shoes."

"I really did want to say something," Coco insisted. "I wanted to tell you that day we had lunch, Elle. But then you mentioned how any woman would be affected by an outside child, and I thought it was best that Aunt Amanda not know."

"I knew there was something going on with you," Elle told her. "You just didn't seem like yourself."

"I guess we need to call an emergency family meeting," Kaitlin said. "I'll send out e-mails as soon as I get home."

"You might just want to make the phone calls," Carrie suggested. "I'm not sure you should sit on this."

Not too long after they left, Ransom walked into the shop. "Coco, do you have a moment?"

She took a quick, sharp breath. "I was just leaving. What about you? What time are you calling it a day?" As their eyes met, she felt a shock run through her.

"I'll follow you to your place."

Coco nodded.

He was definitely upset with her.

"How long have you known that they were my siblings?" Ransom demanded as soon as they walked inside her house.

"I realized it the night we were going through my high school photos," she said quietly. "When did you know?"

"That same night," he said. "When I saw the photos."

"Why didn't you say something to me?" she asked.

"I don't remember you being that forthcoming, either." Folding his arms across his chest, he asked, "Why did you open your mouth this time? That's what I'd like to know."

Her body stiffened in shock. "They wanted to know who you were," Coco said. "What was I supposed to say?"

"Why say anything? If you'd kept your mouth shut, they just would've assumed

148

that I look like their brother. There are people walking around who resemble you, Coco. It doesn't make them family."

"What happened to you wanting to get to know your siblings? You said it was one of the reasons you moved back to Los Angeles."

"None of this was your concern," he told her in a dull and troubled voice. "Who knows what chain of events you've just set off by opening your mouth? You should have left well enough alone."

Coco didn't like his tone and told him so. "Maybe you should leave, Ransom. You know, you really should be grateful to have a family."

"I had a family," he snapped. "They may not have been as perfect as yours, but they were still my family."

Ransom stormed out of the house before she could utter a response.

He's right. I shouldn't have said anything. What have I done? I should have heeded my father's advice. Why couldn't I have just kept my big mouth shut?

Coco felt sick to her stomach.

She wanted to reach out to Ransom once more, but decided to give him as much space as he needed. He could deny it all he wanted, but Coco knew he was afraid.

Ransom was afraid that his newfound family would have no room for him in their lives.

Coco was not the enemy.

Yeah, she should have talked to him first before saying anything to his siblings. It was not her place to get involved in such a sensitive matter. Even if they had pressed her for information, Coco didn't have to tell them anything.

Feeling angry, Ransom smashed his fist into a pillow.

However, he had no right to be so harsh. Deep down, he knew that no matter what she said or didn't say, Coco was only trying to help him.

The doorbell sounded.

He got up and quickly made his way to the front door, wondering who'd come to visit him. He opened it as soon as he realized that Coco was standing outside, and stepped aside to let her enter.

"I know that you're still upset with me," she said. "But I think it's time for us to clear the air. Hopefully we can talk like adults."

They hadn't spoken for two days after the argument at her house.

She followed him into the den.

"I was angry initially," he admitted after they sat down. "I do understand that you only wanted to help me, but I just wished you had come to me first."

"Ransom, I wanted to discuss this with you."

"I owe you an apology for the harshness of my tone. I'm sorry."

"I understand, Ransom." After a brief pause, she asked, "Are you sure it's anger that you feel? Or is it fear?"

"Fear? What are you talking about?"

"Now that they know, they can either embrace you or reject you. I think that's what scares you, Ransom. I think that's why you didn't say anything to me, or try to approach them."

"I don't know which way this is going to turn out for me, but deep down, I'm glad that everything is out in the open finally. Coco, I still don't understand why you didn't tell me that you knew I was related to them."

"I don't know," she responded. "I guess I thought it was best all around not to say anything to you or them. I didn't want to hurt anyone. Ransom, I don't know how the rest of the family is going to react, but Elle and Kaitlin . . . they know the truth and they want to get to know you. You have two sisters who haven't rejected you. Also, my dad urged me to stay out of it and I really respect him and his advice. I always have."

He shook his head. "I still can't believe this is happening."

"I'm sorry, Ransom. I never meant to upset you. I thought I was helping to bring a family together."

"Sweetheart, I'm sorry for the way I snapped at you. I know that you'd never deliberately try to hurt me."

"I love you, Ransom. And no matter what comes out of this, you will always have me."

His kiss was surprisingly gentle.

"I hate that my mother isn't here any longer," he told her. "I think she'd be happy for me. She always regretted not telling my father about me. She said she felt like she did me an injustice. I kept telling her that she wasn't responsible for my choices."

"I don't know about you, but I think we should celebrate," Coco said with a smile.

"What do you have in mind?"

"Ransom, you need a mental break. We could go dancing," she suggested. "It would take your mind off of things for a little while. Have you been to The Purple Door?"

"Once," he said. "Honey, would you mind if we just stay here tonight? I really don't feel like going out." He paused, then murmured, "I've been thinking about Sunday. I don't think I'm going to Riverside. Initially, it sounded like a good idea, but now . . . Honey, I don't know."

"I disagree," Coco replied. "This is what you've always wanted, Ransom. Why are you trying to run away from them?"

"I'm not running away. This is going to change the way they think of their father."

"No, it won't," she countered. "All of the Ransom siblings loved their father, and nothing will ever change that. What's really going on with you?"

"Kaitlin and Elle may welcome me with open arms, but the rest of them might not take it as well. I'm just not ready for all that, Coco."

"You won't know what will happen until we actually go there. Ransom, I love you and I'm not going to let anyone hurt you."

He smiled. "I love you, too."

"You have to see this through," she insisted. "Remember what Kaitlin told you. She vowed they would come to you if you wouldn't go out there."

"It might be better to meet them on my turf."

Coco took his hand in hers. "Ransom, baby, I want you to trust me on this. You are the one who is the risk-taker. You're always telling me that I play it too safe. Well, it's time you followed your own advice."

He gave her a sidelong glance. "So you really think I should go?"

Coco nodded. "I do. It's time you had a chance to get to know your own family."

"I hope you know what you're talking about."

"I'm positive things will go well for you. Ransom, I just believe it — you and your siblings are going to be close."

Coco reached into the huge tote she'd walked in with. "I have something for you."

"What is it?"

"I brought you a box of white-chocolate-covered strawberries and a bottle of non-alcoholic champagne, just in case you nixed the club suggestion. If you don't mind company, we can just sit here and enjoy a movie."

"Thank you," Ransom said. He bit into a strawberry.

"Before I forget, my parents invited us to dinner on Saturday. It's my mom's birthday and the family's getting together at her favorite restaurant."

"This I have no problem doing," he said. "Your parents seem to like me."

"The Ransoms are going to love you as much as I do," Coco declared. "You'll see."

He gave a short laugh before saying, "I

love your optimism."

Coco wrapped her arms around him. "It's going to be fine, Ransom. I can't really explain how I know, but I just do. This is going to work out the way you've always dreamed it would."

"It makes me happy knowing that I have you in my corner."

"Ransom, I will always be here for you. I really care about you."

Her words brought a tiny smile to his lips.

Coco prayed that she wasn't giving Ransom false hope. That would only make the situation worse.

She hadn't talked to Elle or Kaitlin since the whole "outside brother" revelation. Mostly because she was afraid of what they might say. She knew they needed time to process the information, just like Ransom did.

Please let this work out for all of them. Ransom yearns for a relationship with his brothers and sisters. Please give that to him. Please.

She glanced over at him.

Ransom appeared to be engaged in the movie playing on the huge TV screen, but Coco knew better. His mind was on Elle, Kaitlin and the others.

"Do you want to talk about them?" Coco asked. She reached into the tote and pulled out a photo album. "These are pictures that I have of the whole family. There's even some of your dad. This album's for you. I made copies of photos from my other albums."

"I'd like that," Ransom said, looking at her. "Coco, I feel like you're the other part of my soul. Especially since you always seem to know exactly what I need."

She smiled. "I'm your woman. It's my job to anticipate your needs."

Taking her hand in his, Ransom said, "I don't know how my life would be without you. I really love you, Coco."

"Ready?"

He nodded.

"You have ten siblings. I don't know if you knew that already."

"I knew it was a lot. I was thinking five or six. *Ten?*"

She nodded. "You might want to get a pen and paper to write down their names."

Ransom opened a drawer and pulled out a pad and pen. "Ten living?"

Coco laughed. "Yeah, they're all alive."

"That's a lot of children."

"You make eleven."

Stunned, he shook his head.

Coco opened the photo album. "This is your father."

"I have a copy of that picture," Ransom told her. "My mother had it, and she gave it to me when I was around ten. I wanted to know about my dad."

"This is a photo of the entire family. This was taken when they were much younger, though. I think it was the last picture of them together. He died not too long afterward."

"This is his wife? She's beautiful."

"Aunt Amanda is so sweet, Ransom. She and Uncle Prescott were my other parents. He was a good man."

"That's what I've always heard about him . . . Okay, so give me their names," Ransom said.

"This is Prescott Jr., then you have Garret over here," Coco said as she pointed to the photo. "This is Laine and this is Ray."

"He's the U.S. Marshal."

Coco nodded. "This is Ivy. Next to her are Kaitlin and Jillian. This is Nyle. Beside him is Allura. You met Elle. Her name is Rhyan Elle, but she just likes to be called Elle."

"Wow," Ransom murmured, looking at all their faces. "It's a little weird. These are my brothers and sisters."

Coco wrapped her arm around him. "You really should meet them."

He shook his head. "I don't think I'm ready to do that, sweetheart."

"I won't push," she told him, holding up her hands.

"Are they all married?" Ransom inquired.

"Ivy is divorced. The others are still married. Garret's wife, Daisi, has breast cancer. Her percentages are good from what I've heard. They caught it in time."

"They all look so happy."

"They are," Coco said. "They're a strong Christian family, and like you, they try to live their lives according to the Bible."

"I hope that they can survive this," he whispered.

"I'm sure they will," she said. Deep down, Coco shared that same hope. The Ransoms were at their strongest when they were united as a family.

CHAPTER 13

Ransom turned left on Wilshire Boulevard. He and Coco were on their way to her parents' house. They were all going to a restaurant to celebrate Eleanora Stanley's birthday.

"I think your father must have figured it out when we first met," he said as he drove. "I remember he had a strange response to seeing me, but I had no idea why."

"He and Uncle Prescott were close. Dad wasn't surprised when I came to him with my suspicions. He told me then that Uncle Prescott had confided in him. He knew your mother's name, so when he met you all the pieces just fell into place."

Ransom gave her a sidelong glance. "Your dad knew all along, but he didn't say anything?"

"He felt the past should stay in the past. But if the truth came out, he wanted it to happen on its own — which it basically did."

They pulled into the driveway behind Michael's car.

As soon as they walked into the house, Coco's father asked to speak with Ransom alone.

"I'll be out here," she assured him.

The two men went into her dad's office. Daniel sat down behind his desk, while Ransom sat in one of the visitor chairs.

"The reason I asked to speak with you is because Coco told me that the others know about you. I was the one who told my daughter that it was best to keep what she knew to herself."

"I understand that, sir."

"The truth always has a way of coming out," Daniel Sr. said. "Your father was my best friend. He loved God, he loved life and he loved his family. Ransom, he would have loved you, too. I want you to know that."

"Thank you, sir."

"Outside of Amanda, I probably knew him best, so if there is anything you want to know about your father, just come to me."

"Thank you."

Daniel rose to his full height. "Let's not keep our ladies waiting, shall we?"

While they were waiting for her mother to come downstairs, Coco pulled her father into another room. They left Ransom and Michael discussing plans to attend the Super Bowl game in January.

"He does have a lot of the Ransom features," her father whispered. "Lord, have mercy. I wish Prescott were here to meet his son."

Coco agreed. "Kaitlin and Elle want him to come out to Riverside tomorrow to meet everyone, but he doesn't want to go."

"Really? I thought he wanted to meet his family."

"He does, but he's afraid of rejection." She lowered her voice to a whisper, saying, "Daddy, I really hope that they can accept him. Ransom wants this so much. It really bothers him that he didn't get a chance to have a relationship with his dad."

"How is Amanda handling all this?"

"I don't know. I'm sure Elle and Kaitlin told her about him, but I haven't heard from them since."

"I think that he should go out there."

Coco released a soft sigh. "Daddy, I feel that he should go, too, but then it really doesn't matter what I think. This is totally Ransom's decision."

Her father placed an arm around her shoulder. "Give him time, honey."

"I'm trying not to be so pushy."

Daniel Sr. gazed at her, studying her expression. "You seem to care a great deal for this man."

Coco smiled. "I do. Daddy, I'm crazy about him."

"I haven't seen you look this happy in a long time, sweetheart."

"That's because I haven't been," she admitted. "Not like this. Ransom's a good man and I'm glad we found each other."

"Hey, you two plan on joining us for dinner?" Michael asked from the doorway. "People are loading into the car already."

"We're coming."

Coco walked out with her brother.

"Sis, I don't know why I didn't notice it before, but Ransom does look a lot like Laine," Michael said.

"I missed it initially myself," she answered. "It wasn't until we were looking at some old photos that the resemblance hit me."

"You two seem pretty tight these days."

"We are. I really care for him. *A lot.*"

Michael grinned. "Why don't you call it what it really is?" he asked. "You're in love with the guy."

Coco glanced over her shoulder. "Where is Ransom?"

"He's outside already with Daniel. They were talking about the Lakers."

"Daniel's favorite topic," she responded with a laugh. "If they played year-round, that would make my big brother the happiest man in the world."

Michael agreed. "I think he's trying to relive his basketball days through Kobe."

"Daniel was a great basketball player," Coco said. "If he hadn't blown that left knee out, he might still be playing."

"Well, he had three good years with the Lakers," Michael replied.

Coco rushed over to where Ransom and her brother were talking. "It's time to get going," she said. "We need to head to the restaurant if we want to keep our reserved table."

Ransom wrapped an arm around her. "I'm ready, beautiful. Just waiting on you."

Cinnamon ran over to where they were standing. "Can I ride with you, Auntie Coco?"

She glanced up at Ransom, who nodded.

"You sure can, sweetie. Hop in."

"She's adorable," he commented.

"That's my baby," Coco responded as she opened the door for her niece and helped her inside the SUV.

Ransom opened the passenger's-side door for Coco, then walked around and got in on the driver's side. They followed her brother's

Mercedes to the expressway.

"Mr. Ransom, are you my auntie's boy-friend?" Without giving him a chance to respond, she said, "Mommy says that you are. I think that's nice. Auntie's very pretty and she'll be your best girl. I'm my daddy's best girl."

He glanced over at Coco. "You are my best girl."

She was trying hard not to laugh out loud.

"Ooh, Auntie, did you hear him? You *are* his best girl."

Satisfied, Cinnamon turned her attention to the window. She hummed softly to the music playing on the radio as she enjoyed the scenery.

Fifteen minutes later, they were in the parking lot of the restaurant.

They were seated in a private dining room a few minutes after their arrival. Ransom sat beside Coco.

Her father had preselected a menu of wood-grilled salmon, mixed vegetables, rice pilaf and an assortment of rolls.

Coco and her brothers took turns giving tribute to their mother.

"Mama, happy birthday," Coco began. "I want you to know that you are my best friend and I appreciate you so much. I love you."

"I love you, too, baby."

Michael was next. "Mama, you know that I love you and I hope that one day God will bless me with a wife who possesses the same qualities you have. You've set a great example for Coco to follow — for all of us to follow, really. I pray God will allow you to see many more birthdays."

Eleanora smiled. "Thank you, Michael. I love you, too."

Daniel cleared his throat. "Mom, you have been a wonderful role model, as Michael just said. I hope that you are as proud of us as we are of you. I don't think Dad could've asked for a better wife and partner. Our company is a success because of your business acumen, and all of us thank you — and Dad, too — for entrusting us with Stanley Chocolates. I hope that you and Dad will enjoy life and not worry about the business. We won't let you down. Happy birthday and know that I love you."

Their father was the last to speak. "Honey, happy birthday. You know that I adore you. You took my heart captive the first time I saw you, sitting in my father's office. You were all snazzy in that navy blue dress with the gold buttons going down the front. As soon as you left, I went in and demanded that he hire you."

Daniel Sr. reached over and took his wife's hand. "He did, and I think that was the first time he ever listened to me. You were his secretary for, what, six months? And then he promoted you to the sales division. You were our first female sales rep and in your first year doubled our numbers."

Coco loved hearing about how her parents got together. "Mama, why did you refuse to go out with Daddy for so long?"

"I didn't want to mix business with pleasure. My parents had always told me that, so it wasn't until I realized I was in love with him that I turned in my resignation."

Her husband nodded. "That's when I proposed to her. We were engaged for almost a year. She didn't return to the company until after we were married. My father told her that it was the only way he would give his blessing over our marriage."

"He said that sales went down after I left," Eleanora said. "I still don't believe that was true."

"It was," Daniel Sr. insisted. "There were clients who only wanted to deal with you, sweetheart. You had that kind of effect on people. You still do. Ransom, she's the one we call in for our more difficult customers."

Coco nodded. "Mama was the one who fully supported my vision for the chocolate bar. The others . . . they came around, but she was with me from day one."

"I haven't known you that long, Mrs. Stanley," Ransom began. "But I can feel how much you are loved by everyone here. The more I hear, the more I think I'm falling for you myself."

Everyone laughed.

"Seriously, I wish you a very happy birthday and many more."

"Look at our children," Daniel Sr. told his wife. "We have been blessed beyond measure."

Eleanora agreed. "I can still remember when you were all my little babies. Time has just flown by."

"We can always have more," Daniel Sr. said.

"More *what?*" Eleanora asked, while everyone at the table cracked up with laughter.

"I love you enough to have more children."

"Please have a baby," Cinnamon begged. "I want a little girl to play with."

Eleanora slapped her husband on the arm. "Now look what you started." To her granddaughter, Eleanora said, "Honey, I can't have any more babies."

"Are you sure there are no more babies

inside you?" Cinnamon asked. "There might still be one left. Go to the doctor and let him take a look. I bet he'd find another baby."

"Yeah, Mama," Coco said, grinning from ear to ear. "There might be another one. I wouldn't mind a little brother or sister."

"The next baby coming into this family will be from you or Michael," Eleanora replied.

"Your parents are pretty cool," Ransom said when they left the restaurant.

"They are," Coco declared. "We enjoy spending time together as a family like this."

"That's great," Ransom told her. "I can see why your family and my dad's got along so well."

"Have you changed your mind about tomorrow?" she asked.

He gave her a sidelong glance. "You really think I should go out there?"

She nodded. "I'm sure you're sick of discussing it, but Ransom, I really think that you have to go. You need this."

He reached over and took her hand. "I'm going, but I have no real expectations. That way I won't leave disappointed."

"I think that's the best approach," Coco said.

"You're still driving to Riverside with me, right?"

"Of course," she replied. "I wouldn't leave you to deal with this alone."

"Coco, I really feel like a lucky man to have someone like you in my life. I just wanted you to know that."

"I feel the same way about you, Ransom."

He followed Coco into her house thirty minutes later. "I'm picking the movie to-night," he told her. "No more romantic comedies."

"See, I was going to pick an action adven-ture tonight," Coco said. "What do you have in mind?"

"Are we having chocolate or caramel popcorn?" he asked.

"Neither," Coco responded. "Just old-fashioned buttered popcorn."

"Great." Ransom walked over to her DVD library to find a movie. He scanned through her collection until he found something.

He pulled it from the shelf and headed to the sofa, stopping briefly to look at the fam-ily photo on the fireplace mantel. They really were a beautiful family.

Just like the Ransoms.

He wasn't sure if he could truly become a part of that family. Maybe it was just too much to hope for. Ransom swallowed the negative thoughts. Whether they accepted him or not, he was still a member of the family. He was still a Ransom.

Coco walked into the room carrying a bowl of hot buttery popcorn. "Ready?" she asked.

He nodded, then slipped in the movie.

"What did you pick out?" Coco sat down beside him on the red leather sofa.

Ransom held up the DVD jacket. "This one. I haven't seen it, but heard that it was a great film."

"Oh, I like that one," she said. "Good choice."

Ransom wrapped an arm around Coco as they watched the movie. She felt good in his arms, he thought silently. They were a perfect fit.

She fell asleep pressed against him.

Ransom kissed her on the forehead, then leaned his head back against the cushions. He closed his eyes.

"Wha . . ." Coco murmured sleepily. "What time is it?"

Ransom woke up with a start when he felt her move. He glanced down at his watch. "It's four o'clock. I'd better get going."

"You don't have to leave," she protested. "Honey, we can control ourselves. We have so far."

"If you don't mind me sleeping on your couch, I'll stay out here," Ransom said. "You go on to bed."

"Nope. I'm sleeping out here with you."

He stifled a yawn. "Baby, you won't be comfortable."

"Yeah, I will," Coco insisted. "I would rather sleep in your arms on this sofa than in my very comfortable but lonely bed."

Ransom's mouth covered hers hungrily, setting off a wild swirling sensation in her middle. Eventually, she snuggled against him and fell asleep again.

While she dozed, Ransom fought his desire for her and prayed for morning to come. He couldn't sleep, so spent most of the night holding Coco in his arms and playing out various scenarios of what might happen when he arrived at the home his father had shared with his wife and children.

Ransom didn't have any real expectations beyond meeting his siblings. He hadn't liked growing up as an only child — those were lonely years for him. His mother had been an only child herself, so he didn't have any aunts and uncles or cousins.

He knew that his father had come from a fairly large family, so that he must have a host of relatives on the paternal side that he had never met. Ransom hoped to change all that because, when the time came for him to marry, he didn't want his side of the church empty. And he wanted any children he fathered to know their relatives.

He was grateful to have Coco in his life. And now that everything was out in the open, Ransom could be totally honest with her about his feelings. It had taken the weight of the world off his shoulders, being able to confide in her.

She was very optimistic about this visit to Riverside. Ransom decided to adopt a wait-and-see attitude. He was going to have to face eleven people, and was pretty sure not all of them were going to welcome him with open arms.

CHAPTER 14

When she woke up at 6:00 a.m. Coco noted that Ransom looked as if he hadn't slept at all, so she convinced him to climb into her bed to get some sleep.

She didn't wake him until noon.

Yawning, Ransom sat up in bed.

"I made breakfast," Coco announced. "You can use this robe if you want to take a shower."

"I have some sweats in the car," Ransom said.

"You go shower and I'll get the sweats. I'll leave them on the bed in here."

Ransom came downstairs and joined her in the kitchen fifteen minutes later.

Coco fixed a plate and handed it to him.

He sat down, closed his eyes and said grace over the food.

She took a sip of her cranberry juice, surveying his face. He didn't look as tired as he had earlier. A few hours' sleep and a shower had done wonders for him.

Ransom looked up and asked, "Baby, what time should we head out to Riverside?"

"I'd say around two-thirty. With traffic, it's going to take us at least an hour to get there."

He nodded. "After you get dressed, we'll stop by my place so that I can change."

"Okay," she murmured between bites.

He couldn't keep his eyes off Coco.

There was something so intimate in spending the night with the woman you loved. There was physical intimacy, but what he had shared with Coco was an emotional intimacy. He was in love with her.

Ransom cleaned the kitchen while she went to get ready. He forced his mind on to washing dishes instead of wondering what Coco looked like in various states of undress.

He had just finished sweeping up when she came out of her bedroom. "I'm ready," she announced, then scanned her gourmet kitchen. "Nice job, Ransom."

"I have many hidden talents," he responded with a grin.

"I bet you do," she murmured.

"Girl, you make it hard on a brother . . ."

Coco laughed. "What are you talking about, Ransom? I haven't done a thing."

His lips slowly descended to meet hers and she felt her knees weaken.

"We'd better get going," she whispered.

Ransom agreed. "It's time to meet the family."

Coco gave him a reassuring hug.

"Why are you so quiet?" she asked as they entered the 405 Freeway en route to the 110. "Are you still nervous about meeting your brothers and sisters? You really shouldn't be. They are all very nice."

"Yeah, I am," he admitted. "I don't like bringing drama into their lives like this. Coco, I don't know what I was thinking. I never should have agreed to it."

"Ransom, you want a relationship with your siblings. I've known this family for a long time. Your father and my dad were best friends. Will you please trust me on this?"

"Why do you feel that everyone is going to be so accepting? Do you know something I don't know?"

"I just know this family and how loving they are. Family means everything to them. You're very lucky to have been born a Ransom."

"Why didn't you ever say anything to me?" he asked quietly. "If they are so great, then why keep quiet?"

"Ransom, I care a great deal for you and I

didn't want to get your hopes up. It would've devastated you and I couldn't risk that. I did go to my dad and ask him if he knew anything."

"He told me that he suspected it the moment he met me."

Coco nodded. "Apparently your father confided in mine. Dad knew all about your mother, even the fact that Prescott cared for her. But he loved Miss Amanda and he wanted to be with her and his children."

"Sometimes I wonder what would've happened if he had known my mother was pregnant." Ransom checked his rearview and side mirrors before merging onto the Pomona Freeway.

"I think that he would have been a part of your life, but he still would have gone back to Miss Amanda," Coco said gently.

"I believe that you're right."

"How does that make you feel?" she asked.

"I really would have liked a chance to get to know him, have a relationship with him and my siblings."

"I'm so glad you're going to finally get the opportunity to meet them."

"I'm still not sure this is the right thing to do, sweetheart."

"If things take a turn for the worse, I'll get you out of there," Coco promised. "But,

176

Ransom, I have every confidence that this is going to go well."

He smiled. "I love that you're so optimistic."

"I've known this family for a really long time and they will welcome you with open arms — I'm sure of it. Your oldest brother, Prescott, and his family flew in yesterday because he wants to meet you."

"I bet Ray and Matt had me investigated already." He gave a slight shrug. "It's fine because I don't have anything to hide."

To ease his mind, Coco changed the subject to music. "Did you finish the song you were working on?"

Ransom gave her a sidelong glance. "Almost," he answered.

"Can you tell me about it?"

"It's a love song."

"What happens after you write it?" Coco asked curiously. "Do you have someone record it?"

"I've already sold it," he said. "I was commissioned by Adela to write a love song for her. We've worked together on all of her previous albums."

"I think I remember her thanking you during one of the Grammy shows. She had just won one and she thanked you for writing the song that was honored."

"You're right," Ransom said. "She won for 'That Love.' "

"Wow!" Coco exclaimed. "So you wrote 'That Love'? It's a beautiful song."

"She made it beautiful. Before, it was just words."

He got off at the next exit and turned right.

"Make the next left," Coco told him.

Following her directions, Ransom slowly pulled to a stop and turned off the car in front of a two-story French-style home. The house was a picture of enchantment with the striking Palladian window. Two huge, healthy looking ferns sat on either side of the front door.

"Ready?" she asked, taking Ransom's hand in hers.

He shook his head.

She hugged him. "C'mon . . . let's go inside. Your family's waiting for you."

Ransom glanced around. "Look at all these cars. It's like a parking lot out here."

"You do have a huge family."

"Lord, give me strength," he whispered.

A woman walked out on the porch. Ransom noted she walked with the assistance of a cane.

"Oh, my goodness," she said as they came closer. "You have a lot of Prescott in you."

"Aunt Amanda, this is Ransom Winters," Coco said.

"It's so good to meet you, Ransom." Amanda gave Coco a hug. "And it's always a pleasure to see my girl. I don't see you much anymore, since Elle got married. I'm still here."

Coco chuckled. "Yes, ma'am. I'll do much better by you, Aunt Amanda."

Kaitlin walked outside. "Ransom, I'm glad you came. I was about to round up the clan and head your way."

He laughed.

She didn't crack a smile. "No, I'm serious."

He glanced at Coco, who shrugged and said, "You heard her. She's telling you the truth."

"Coco was the one who convinced me to come today."

Kaitlin smiled then. "I'm glad you're here. My . . . our oldest brother and his family flew in from Michigan last night so that they could meet you."

"I take it everyone else lives locally."

"All over Los Angeles," Kaitlin responded. "Allura is the only one of us who still lives in Riverside. She and her family live in the next block. C'mon, I think it's time you met the others."

When he walked inside the house, a woman met him in the hallway, her eyes quickly assessing him. "You must be Ransom." She held out her hand. "Hello, I'm Ivy. I'm your oldest sister. I was born after Prescott Jr."

Ransom shook her hand, noting her firm grip and her direct gaze. "It's nice to meet you, Ivy."

Coco pulled out her camera. She wanted to capture every moment for Ransom. She was going to present all of the photos in a nice album for him.

Ivy took a surprised Ransom by the arm. "Let me introduce you to everyone else."

He certainly wasn't expecting such a warm reception. Coco saw the stunned expression on his face.

"Ransom, I'm Jillian," another woman said. "Ivy is the bossy one."

"And Jillian is the very straightforward sister — she can cut you with the truth if you're not careful," Ivy responded.

He gave a polite chuckle. "I think I can handle that."

A man sitting in one of the wing chairs stood up and said, "I'm Prescott, and this lovely lady is my wife, Cheryl."

"He's the oldest," Jillian explained. "After Ivy is my . . . *our* brother Garret."

Ransom met Garret's gaze and said, "You own the funeral home, right?"

He nodded. "Forgive me for staring, but you look so much like my father and Laine. This is my wife, Daisi."

They were joined by another man who said, "I'm Laine and I have to agree. We do resemble each other. It's freaky in a way."

A woman held up her hand. "I'm Regis and I'm married to Laine."

Ransom broke into a grin and said, "One thing I see is that all of the men in this family have great taste in women."

Laine laughed. "A man who appreciates beauty. He's definitely one of us."

"Hey, we Ransom women haven't done too shabbily, either," Jillian said. Pointing to the man beside her, she said, "This is my extremely handsome hubby, John."

"Except for me," Ivy muttered. "I went fishing and came home with a shark. I'm divorced."

Ransom could see that it still pained her.

Without thinking, he pulled her in his arms and gave her a hug. "It's his loss, and maybe God had to clear him out of the way for your prince to come."

She looked him straight in the eyes and said, "I don't need any kind of test to tell me that this man is my brother. He has our heart. My father would've said something like that."

"That's exactly what he would've said," Amanda interjected.

Another man came forward. "Ransom, I'm Ray, and you've already met my wife, Carrie. You'll meet all of the children later. We wanted to spend some time with you before saying anything to them."

"I understand completely," he replied.

"Hey, Ransom, I'm Allura," a young woman interjected from the doorway. "I'm between Laine and Kaitlin. This is Trevor . . . my husband."

Ransom glanced over at the young man sitting near the door.

"I'm Nyle and this is my wife, Chandra. I've been trying to figure out exactly where you fit into this family. When were you born?"

"It had to be in 1976 or '77," Amanda answered before he could respond. "That was the only time your father and I were separated."

"I was born in 1976," Ransom confirmed. "I want you all to know that I'm not looking for anything from any of you. I've always wanted to know my father and to meet my siblings. I've done that and so I thank you. I'll also understand if this is too uncomfortable for you."

Ray shook his head. "Ransom, it's not that simple, man. I'm the first to admit that I was skeptical, but seeing you now . . . I know the truth."

"But how do you feel about it?"

"It's a bit weird for me," Ray admitted. "But before our father died, he made us promise that we would always be there for one another. He always stressed the importance of family. I'm not going to blemish his memory by turning my back on you."

"We all feel the same way as Ray," Prescott said.

Nyle rose to his feet and said, "I'm sorry, but I'm not entirely convinced that he is truly one of us."

"I'm willing to take a DNA test."

"That won't do it for me," Nyle responded.

Ransom glanced over at Coco, confused.

"We need to see you on the basketball court. I hope you brought balling clothes with you."

Ransom smiled. "I always keep some in the car."

"I don't know about the rest of you all, but I'm watching this game," Chandra said.

"So am I," Coco declared.

The other women agreed.

Soon everyone was gathered outside in the backyard.

"Kids, we need the court," Prescott said to the children, who immediately ran off to the sides. "This isn't going to take long," he assured them.

"Can Ransom play?" Elle asked in a low voice.

Coco nodded. "He plays well."

She grinned. "I knew it. He's definitely my brother."

"So what do you boys think now?" Ivy asked as they walked off the court an hour later. "Because from where I was standing, it looked like Ransom dominated the game."

"He's got skills," Ray responded, after trying to catch his breath. "I'll give him that. The man can play some ball."

Ransom followed the others off the court. "Seriously, I am very willing to take a DNA test. I don't blame you for wanting to make sure. I would if I were in your shoes."

"Ransom, I don't need a DNA test. My husband told me about Robina Winters," Amanda said. "She was your mother. The only reason he didn't tell me about you is because I'm sure he had no idea she was pregnant. She moved away after they broke up, and to my knowledge, he never spoke to her again."

"That's right," Ransom said, knowing there was no way she could know all that without it being true. "Miss Amanda, I'm certain this has to bother you in some way."

"Honey, it doesn't," she assured him. "I know that your father loved me with his whole heart. Prescott was good to me and was only unfaithful while we were separated, as far as I know. We laid that to rest long ago and so I have a peace about it. Your father is gone and I regret that he did not get a chance to meet you, but know this, Ransom. You are as much my family as your father was. If you let me, I'm willing to be in your life. I'm not trying to replace your mother, but just know that you have me."

He grinned. "I'd like that, Miss Amanda."

"Welcome to the family," Prescott said.

One by one, they came up and embraced him.

Coco wiped a tear from her eye.

The children were just as excited to meet their new uncle, especially Kaitlin's daughter Travaille. She stayed by his side when she wasn't in his lap.

"He really has a heart for kids," Elle said to Coco, who nodded in agreement.

"So how serious is this between you two?"

Coco shrugged. "I don't know. We're just kind of taking it one day at a time."

Elle laughed. "Okay, you've given me the politically correct answer. Now tell me the real deal."

"I think he's the one, Elle."

"That's great! Hey, do you remember when you couldn't stand him because of all the hip-hop music coming from his center, and all the teens hanging around the place?"

"Just say it," Coco said. "I was an idiot."

"Well, at least you've come to your senses."

"Yeah," she agreed. "If I hadn't, I would've missed out on a wonderful man."

"I am so blown away by what happened today," Ransom said when they were on the way back to Los Angeles. "I really enjoyed hanging out with them. These people are my brothers and sisters . . . all of them. Miss Amanda — she's incredible. My mom always said that she was a nice woman. She was right."

"Did they know each other?"

"I don't think so," Ransom said. "But apparently, my dad was very up front with both of them."

"I think that's admirable, but I'm not really surprised by this," Coco said. "He really was a nice man."

"I believe that. He just wasn't in love with

my mother, but she loved him. There was never another man for her."

Coco remained silent.

"It's okay. He was honest with her, so my mother knew what she was getting into. I don't blame him for anything."

They arrived at the house, got out of the car and went inside. Ransom sat down on the living room sofa beside her. "Thanks so much for going with me, Coco. If it hadn't been for you I don't think I would have gone."

"I'm glad it worked out the way that it did," she told him. "It's what I was praying for."

"Me, too," Ransom acknowledged. "I hope I won't scare you away when I say this, but I think you need to know something."

She studied his lean, dark face. "Ransom, what is it?"

"I want to make lots of babies with you."

The very air around her seemed electrified. "Define 'lots of babies,' " she responded.

"Three or four."

A wave of relief washed over her and she smiled. "I guess I can handle that, but you know that before the baby making part, there needs to be a ring on my finger."

He laughed. "You're right about that. I

don't want to bring a child into this world without marriage. My mother worked hard until the day she died. She and my grandmother did the best they could for me, but I want my children to have both parents. This is one of the reasons I'm celibate — other than the fact that I'm a Christian. I didn't want to risk an unplanned pregnancy." Ransom's eyes traveled her face. "Although I have to confess you have me rethinking my celibacy."

"Stay strong," she said with a short laugh.

"You make it hard on a brother, Coco."

"Naw," she responded. "I'm just a reminder that you're human."

"More like a reminder that I'm a man."

"Baby, what can I do to ease your pain?" Ransom groaned.

Coco laughed.

CHAPTER 15

The summer months passed quickly.

The new school year had started and Ransom already had two boys who'd managed to get themselves suspended during the first week of school.

Over the course of the summer, Ransom had spent a lot of time getting to know his siblings. He seemed really happy and that thrilled Coco. She was beyond grateful to be able to see him like this. She had begun taking her digital camera with her whenever they were all together. She wanted to capture those special times for Ransom.

He and Coco joined the rest of the family for the fall festival at the church Laine and Regis attended.

"You guys made it!" Elle exclaimed in delight when she spotted them. She gave them each a hug. At seven months pregnant, Elle was glowing and beautiful.

"Travaille has been looking for you," she

told Ransom. "Oh, I have to tell you that Matt's broken up over the fact that he's no longer the center of his daughter's universe."

"He still is," Ransom said. "He is all she really talks about."

"Do you think that maybe you could tell him that?" Elle asked with a soft chuckle. "I'm tired of seeing him walking around looking like he's lost his best friend."

Ransom gave a slight nod. "I'd be more than happy to tell him. I wouldn't dream of taking his place. Travaille loves her daddy, and believe me, he's her world."

When Elle went in search of her twin boys, Coco told Ransom, "You're *my* world."

"And you're mine."

Some of the children talked Ransom into going on rides with them.

Amusement park rides were not her thing, so Coco sat down beside Elle and Kaitlin whenever she wasn't taking pictures.

"Have you and Ransom discussed taking your relationship to the next level?" Kaitlin asked.

"Next level . . . Are you talking sex or marriage?"

"Marriage."

Coco shook her head. "Not really. Ransom and I know that we love each other. We've been together since April, and I'm not rushing anything. I would rather it happen naturally."

"I'm glad Ransom came into our lives," Kaitlin said. "I really like him and I'm glad he's my brother."

"I feel the same way," Elle stated. "The children all adore him and he's very good with them."

Coco agreed. "That's his passion."

Kaitlin rubbed the round mound of her belly. Her baby wasn't due for another three months. "Seems like Ransom's teen center is doing very well. I read the article in the paper. They did an outstanding job."

"Now with two centers open, he's running himself ragged. He's interviewing for a director for the Inglewood Center. Ransom's being very picky and for good reason. He wants to bring in the right person for the teens."

"I can certainly understand that," Kaitlin declared.

Ransom walked over to where they were sitting. "Hey, beautiful," he said to Coco.

She smiled up at him. "Hey yourself."

"Are you having a good time?"

She nodded. "The best."

"Why don't we go find something to drink?" he suggested.

Coco rose to her feet. "I'll follow you,"

They stayed at the festival for another hour before calling it a night. Ransom had some paperwork he needed to complete by morning. They located their family members and said their goodbyes.

"Ransom, I can't tell you how much it thrills me to see you with your family like this," Coco told him on the drive home. "I never tire of seeing you all together."

"It's an answer to my prayer, that's for sure," he told her. "I have you and my family — I don't need anything else."

"What's this?" Ransom asked when Coco handed him a shiny black-and-white gift bag.

"You have to open it and see," she responded with a chuckle.

He pulled out a gift-wrapped box, then ripped off the paper. "It's a photo album." He read the label. "Ransom Family Memories . . . sweetheart, this is nice."

She opened it to the first page. "These are the photos I took when we went to Riverside, and the ones from Friday night at the festival. I want you to have memories from all of your Ransom family get-togethers."

"I hadn't realized you took so many the day we were in Riverside. This is great,

Coco. Thank you."

She pointed to a photograph. "Remember that one? That's when you made your third three-pointer."

He laughed. "Look at Ray's face."

Coco chuckled. "He was hoping you were going to make the shot. This was the winning basket."

"Matt and Nyle made most of the points for their team. On our team, Ray's and John's shots weren't hitting. We needed that one."

"It was a good game."

He agreed. "We're getting together next weekend for a game."

"That's great," Coco said, pleased that he and his brothers were bonding.

"I have to get back to work," Ransom said. "I need to process some paperwork for the students coming in on Monday."

"You can send one of them over here to perform community service for a couple of hours," Coco offered.

"Really?"

She nodded. "I'm sure you'll send one over who isn't a hardened criminal."

"You're right about that. Thanks, honey. There aren't enough businesses signed up for the number of kids I get coming in each week."

"A friend of mine owns the ice cream shop in the next block. I'll give her a call and see if you can meet with her."

"Sweetheart, that would be great," Ransom said. "The more companies I can get to join us, the more opportunities for my students to see the types of jobs available to them. I'm hoping that something will spark a real interest in each of them."

Coco picked up the phone and dialed. She talked with her friend for a few minutes, then hung up. "Brenda says she can see you now if you'd like to meet with her."

Ransom stood up. "Perfect," he said.

"Ricky, this is Miss Stanley," Ransom said, making introductions. "You'll come here for the next three days to do community service. She'll have a list of tasks for you to complete over the course of two hours."

"What I'm gon' do in this place?" he asked, a frown on his face.

"Sweep the floors, clean the stockroom and restock the shelves for me," Coco said. "It's not hard work, but it's time consuming."

Ricky met her gaze. "I ain't afraid of hard work, ma'am."

Coco glanced at Ransom, who said, "That's good to hear, Ricky. That's what it takes to make it in this world."

"Are you ready to get started?" she asked.

"Just point me to the broom closet and I'll take it from there," Ricky said.

There was something about his demeanor that was different from the other boys she'd encountered at the center. Maybe it was because this was their first meeting, or maybe he thought she was like some of the other adults he'd encountered — the ones who didn't care or showed no interest in him as a person.

"I'll be back in a couple of hours," Ransom said.

He left the two of them alone. Coco was grateful that Bryan and Valencia were working with her.

Although Ricky didn't seem to have much in the personality department, he swept the shop floor and did an excellent job of it. Next he swept the floor in the stockroom and cleaned the bathroom.

She broke into a smile when Valencia came out singing his praises.

Coco offered him a soda.

"Thank you," he replied, accepting the cold drink. "Your place is nice. This is real nice."

"It's a dream come true for me," she told

him. "And it took a lot of hard work to get here."

"I can believe that," he said. "I'ma have my own business one day."

"I wouldn't be surprised," Coco said. "Ricky, it can happen for you just like it did for me."

"You one of them Stanleys," he responded. "You got a lot of money attached to your name. It ain't like that for me."

"What type of business would you like to have?" she asked.

"I don't know," he answered with a shrug.

Something about Ricky bothered her, but Coco couldn't put her finger on what. She decided to keep her eye on him for the duration of his time with her.

One of the other boys, who had gotten suspended along with Ricky, walked into the shop. He introduced himself. "My name is Marcus. I've been over there working with your brother. I feel like I've gained weight surrounded by so much chocolate."

Coco smiled. "It does feel that way sometimes."

He made conversation while they waited for Ransom or one of the other staff members to come get them.

"It's right across the street," Ricky was saying. "Why can't we just walk back when we get finished? I don't need no babysitter."

"Man, chill . . ." Marcus told him. "They have certain rules and we got to follow them. We ain't heard nothing but good things about D-Unit. Mr. Winters, he got our backs, so we can do this. Okay?"

Amused, Coco dropped her eyes, noting the custom basketball shoes Marcus was wearing. They were similar to the ones Daniel ordered.

How can he afford shoes like that? she wondered. Then she realized that not all of the teens that had been suspended lived in impoverished neighborhoods.

Ricky nodded.

I like Marcus, she thought silently. Ricky was okay, but she didn't quite trust him.

Coco didn't say anything to Ransom about what she was feeling. She had no proof of anything and didn't want to be guilty of prejudging the teen. Besides, it was only two more days. She would just keep a close eye on him.

CHAPTER 16

"Ransom, there was another robbery last night not too far from here," Coco told him. For the past week, robberies were being reported in the newspaper. They had started around the first of October.

He nodded. "I heard about it when I was coming to work this morning."

"The news reporters are saying that it's a gang."

He met her gaze. "Do you think it's some of my students?"

"How do you know it's not?" she asked, thinking of Ricky. During the three days he'd worked in the shop, Coco had heard him on numerous occasions asking Valencia a lot of questions about the business, such as if it made a lot of money. He had been gone for a few weeks now, but she still thought he might be behind the robberies.

"Honey, it's not my boys," Ransom said.

"I didn't want to say anything, but I think

you should know. There was something about Ricky that bothered me."

Ransom's expression suddenly became guarded. "What?"

"I can't really put my finger on it, but he just didn't seem right. He kept asking Valencia if the store made a lot of money, if we had an alarm system. Stuff like that."

Ransom folded his arms across his chest. "So you think he's the one doing this?"

"He is a member of a gang," Coco reminded him. "That was part of the reason he got suspended from school."

"He's a wannabe gang member," Ransom said. "There's a difference."

"That would make him more dangerous, don't you think?"

"Coco, the boy is back in school and doing well."

"Why are you angry with me?" she asked.

"Because you've decided, with no evidence whatsoever, that Ricky is out committing robberies. You know what? I'm not going to send another boy over there."

"Ransom, that's not what I'm saying."

"I'd like to think I'm a good judge of character, Coco. Do you honestly think that I'd send someone to you who could potentially cause you harm?"

"You don't know these boys, Ransom,"

Coco argued. "Not really." She didn't want to fight with him, but she needed to open his eyes. Some of the boys he had to deal with were nothing but trouble.

"I know them better than you do."

"Ransom, you won't be able to save them all. You only had Ricky for three days. Did you really think you could rehabilitate him in that short period of time?"

Valencia came through the front door and called out a greeting.

Ransom stepped down off the bar stool. "I need to get to the center."

Coco glared at him.

He walked briskly toward the door.

They were supposed to have lunch together, but when she didn't hear from him by noon, Coco walked over to the factory.

"What's wrong, sis?" Michael asked.

"Ransom and I had a fight."

"Are you okay?"

She nodded. "He refuses to believe that those students of his could possibly revert back to their old ways."

Michael looked puzzled. "Come again?"

"The string of robberies, Michael," Coco said. "I really think it could be one of the boys from the center."

"Why would you think that?" he asked.

"These boys are coming into our businesses, performing community service, but what else are they doing? They could be casing the place. Remember Ricky?"

Michael nodded.

"That's what I think he was doing. He was asking too many questions about my shop."

"Sis, I don't know about this. I think you may be jumping to conclusions here. You weren't robbed and Ricky only worked with you."

She hadn't really considered that point.

"Do you think that he and Marcus are doing this?" Michael asked. "They weren't the only two in the program within the last month. How can you single out one boy?"

"I guess I hadn't fully thought it through," Coco said. "No wonder Ransom is so upset with me." She rose to her feet. "I need to go over there to apologize."

Coco hugged her brother, then rushed out of the building.

She released a short sigh of relief upon seeing Ransom's SUV in the reserved parking space.

One of the staff members greeted her when she walked inside.

"Is Ransom busy? I'd like to talk to him," she said.

"You can head straight back," the man told her.

Coco knocked on the open door.

Ransom looked up.

"Can I come in?" she asked.

He nodded. "I don't want to keep rehashing this, Coco."

"We're not," she said as she closed the door behind her. "Ransom, I came over here to apologize to you. I admit that Ricky spooked me a little, but I had no right to just accuse him of committing a crime like that."

"Ricky does have a criminal record," he told her. "But the last couple of years, he's either been walking the straight and narrow or he just hasn't been caught."

"Ricky only worked with me, so I guess he couldn't have done this."

"There's always a possibility, Coco, but I just don't think he's the one doing this."

"You don't want to think the worse of them," she said. "I understand that."

"I wouldn't send someone over there who —"

"Ransom, I know that," Coco interjected, cutting him off. "I know that you'd protect me with your life."

"Why didn't you tell me?"

"About Ricky and the way I felt around him?" she shrugged. "I wanted to make sure that it wasn't me being judgmental. But the truth is I just didn't trust him."

"I'm sorry," he said.

She smiled. "So am I."

Coco headed to the door. "I need to get back to the shop. See you later?"

"I have a meeting in Inglewood. I'll be leaving here around four. I'll catch up with you later on tonight." Ransom got up and came around his desk. "I love you, Coco, and I would never place you in harm's way."

"I know that," she told him.

He kissed her.

"I wish I could stay here in your arms, but my assistant manager is probably starving. I need to get back."

"I'll walk you over," Ransom said.

"You get back to work," Coco insisted. "I can make it back to the shop on my own. Oh, you still owe me lunch."

"Can I make it up to you tomorrow?" he asked.

"Definitely."

Coco walked back into her shop with a big smile on her face.

She relieved Valencia for lunch.

When her assistant manager returned, the two women restocked the shelves between waiting on customers for the rest of the afternoon.

■ ■ ■ ■

Elle gave birth to a little girl on the fifth of November.

Coco was there with camera in hand to record the blessed event. "She's gorgeous," she told her exhausted friend.

"Thank you. She really is beautiful, isn't she?"

Before Coco could utter a response, Elle had fallen asleep.

Ransom eased into the hospital room.

"She's sleep," Coco whispered. "She's exhausted."

He tiptoed out again, with Coco following behind him.

"Brennan is down at the nursery with the baby."

"I'll go down there in a few. What are you about to do?" Ransom asked.

"I need to get to the shop. I'm closing tonight."

"So are you leaving now?" he inquired.

Coco nodded. "Yeah, I have to relieve Bryan for lunch. Valencia's on vacation this week."

"I'm going to hang around here for a little while. See if Elle wakes up anytime soon," Ransom told her. "Then I have to go to

Beverly Hills for a meeting. I probably won't make it by the center today."

She smiled. "I'm sure your staff has everything under control."

"They do," he said. "I only have one kid this week."

"Wow. That's a good thing, right?"

"I think so."

She kissed him. "Well, I've got to get out of here. Tell everyone bye for me."

"Have a good day, baby."

"I'm going to do my best."

By the time Coco made it to her car, it was raining.

That's just great, she thought. It had started out such a pretty day until the dark clouds settled in.

Rain poured down, creating puddles all over the parking lot. Using an old newspaper to shield her short hair, Coco stepped away from a puddle gathered on the corrugated black rubber mat just outside the door.

Running her fingers through rain-damp hair, she gazed upon row after row of shelves displaying gift baskets, candy treats and other products under the fluorescent lighting of the shop. There were a handful of browsers walking around, a couple of them holding bags of candy and other gift items.

Coco spied Bryan standing behind the counter talking to one of their customers. She waved to him on her way to the office in the rear of the shop. Coco quickly brushed her teeth and touched up her makeup before trying to salvage her hair. Then she went to work.

A customer burst through the front door just then, pausing briefly to shake the droplets from her raincoat. After propping her umbrella in a corner, she moved to peruse the items on sale.

Bryan walked briskly over to where she was standing and greeted the woman politely.

She glanced around and said, "I've never been in here before. The store is really nice."

"Thank you," he and Coco replied in unison.

"We have some samples of our products on the bar," Coco told the woman. She bit back a smile when the customer zoomed in on the basket of goodies.

"Oh, my goodness," she exclaimed. "This is delicious. I've got to get some."

Bryan left the sales floor and walked behind the bar to further assist her. Coco could hear him explaining the process of how the candy was made and answering her other questions.

"What else can I get for you, Misty?" Coco heard him ask her. He made a few more suggestions while Coco went to assist another customer who'd just entered the store.

After the shoppers left, Bryan turned to Coco, saying, "It's pouring down rain and customers are pouring in here today. What's up with that?"

"I'll take them any way I can get them," she said with a chuckle. He was right, though. Usually when it was raining heavily like this, traffic was low, but not today.

They had two more customers walk in.

For the better part of the afternoon, Coco and Bryan stayed busy, until he clocked out shortly after four.

Coco had three customers between the time Bryan left and closing. Shortly before six o'clock, the door opened and three men walked into the shop with caps pulled low, covering most of their faces.

Coco felt a chill go down her spine. She had forgotten to lock the door. Thank goodness she had given the deposit to Bryan when he left.

"I'm sorry, but we're closed," she said as calmly as she could manage.

"Looks like you're open to me," the tallest of the trio said. "We just walked through the door." He laughed.

I wish I'd installed a panic button under the bar like Michael suggested. What to do . . . what to do.

Coco tried to remain calm so that she could think.

"What would you like?" she asked, then instantly regretted it.

"All of your cash," the man said, pulling out a gun and pointing it straight at her.

"Just do it, Miss Stanley," the one near the door shouted.

He knows me. He's one of the boys from the center. Was it Ricky? She really couldn't tell because the boy had made a conscious effort to disguise his voice.

"Shut up," the one with the gun ordered. "Don't you say nothing else."

He sounded much older and was much bigger than the other two. Coco surmised that he was the leader in this scenario.

"I don't keep a lot of cash in the store," she told him.

The boy in the back moved closer and his shoes caught her eye. Coco felt a sense of dread.

Marcus.

"I'm not gonna say it again. Give me all

of your cash."

The door swung open and Coco caught a glimpse of her brother, Benjamin and Jerome. Things went awry after that.

Coco screamed when she heard the gun go off.

She saw her brother falling and Benjamin wrestling with the man with the gun.

"Call the police!" Jerome shouted as he peered outside.

She glanced around the room, looking for Marcus, but he was gone, along with the other teen.

Jerome assisted Benjamin in subduing the leader facedown on the floor. Then Benjamin kicked the gun across the room.

Coco heard sirens in the distance and rushed over to where her brother was lying, cringing at the sight of so much blood. "Michael!"

"It's just my arm," he said. "He shot me in the arm."

The shop was soon overflowing with paramedics and police.

Numbed from the shock of what had taken place, Coco rode to the hospital with her brother.

Jerome and Benjamin insisted on meeting her there.

"I called Mr. Winters," Benjamin announced when they arrived. "He's gonna come here. Everything gonna be fine."

Ransom was the last person she wanted to see.

Ransom found Coco sitting in the lobby of the emergency room. He sat down beside her, saying, "I got here as soon as I could."

"My brother was shot," she said without looking at him.

"Benjamin told me. I'm so sorry."

Coco looked up at him then, her eyes cold. "You're sorry? My brother could've been killed tonight and you're sorry."

He was thrown by the way she was treating him. Ransom assumed she was still in shock. "Look, I know that you're upset. Did the doctor check you out?"

"I don't need to see a doctor," she snapped. "Ransom, I have every right to be angry. Remember how you told me that it wasn't one of your boys? Well, you were wrong."

"Ricky?"

She shook her head. "It was Marcus. When he came over to the shop, I noticed his custom Nikes and I wondered how he was able to afford such expensive shoes. Well, now I know. Only he isn't very smart. He had them on tonight."

Ransom's hands balled into fists.

"I told you that you couldn't save all of them. I moved to Brentwood to escape stuff like this."

"Any time you run a retail business, you run the risk of being robbed, Coco."

"That risk is even higher with your center being in the neighborhood."

He looked as if she had stabbed him in the heart. "Where do you think these boys live, Coco? They attend schools in this area. They live around here."

"Why don't you relocate your center somewhere else? Put it in the hood — that's where they belong. Let them fight it out, rob or whatever they do there anyway."

"I realize you're upset, Coco, but you have no right to tell me where I should build a center. If you're so unhappy, then *you* relocate. But unless you move to an uninhabited island, you will run the risk of this happening again."

Ransom rose to his feet. "I am sorry this happened to you. I'm doubly sorry that it was one of my students, but I'm not moving D-Unit. I'm taking Benjamin and Jerome with me now because I won't risk you destroying them with your venom."

Coco put a hand to her face. "I . . . Ransom . . ."

"I can't talk to you anymore. One minute you are super supportive and then when something goes wrong you show what you're really about. You are just like some of the other people who run around judging these kids by what they see on the outside. Me, I look at the inside. Even God tells us that He doesn't look at our externals — but at our heart. When I look at these boys, I see their heart, Coco. Marcus slipped through the cracks and I'm going to find out what can be done." Ransom sighed in resignation. "I'll give Michael a call to see how he's doing."

"Ransom, wait," Coco said.

"I have to get these boys home."

He gestured for Jerome and Benjamin to come with him. "I'm taking you home."

"You okay, Mr. Winters?" Jerome asked.

He nodded. "I'm fine."

He was so disappointed in Marcus. The boy seemed to have a lot of potential, but he wasn't strong enough to stay away from the gang, as he'd promised. Ransom had pegged him as more of a follower, which was why he'd spent so much time talking to the boy.

He swallowed his hurt. *I thought I'd reached him. I was wrong, and now I've lost the woman I love most in this world.*

Coco was ashamed of the way she'd attacked Ransom the night Michael was shot. That was two weeks ago. She was too embarrassed to call him, and she knew he wouldn't call her.

Valencia walked into the shop and handed her an envelope. "One of the staff members from D-Unit asked me to deliver this to you."

Coco frowned. "What is it?"

"I don't know. He was on his way over here when he saw me getting out of the car. He just asked me to bring it to you."

She took it with her to her office.

Inside were a letter and a ten-dollar bill.

Miss Stanley:

I am so sorry for what I did. I didn't mean or want to hurt you or your brother. I know that you probably recognized me that night and that you hate me. I don't blame you if you do. I didn't want to steal from you, but my big brother (the one with the gun) made me do it.

I hope that one day you can forgive me. Mr. Winters comes to visit me and I apologized to him. I asked him to bring you so that I can say I'm sorry to your face, but since you haven't come, I guess that means that you really hate me.

I only have ten dollars and I wanted you to have it. It's my way of showing you that I'm serious. I will pay you back for all the damages we caused. I am probably going to get some jail time and that scares me. I hope that you will forgive me and pray for me. For my safety. You're probably saying that you used to feel safe until that night.

I pray that you never go through something like that again. I am really sorry. Please don't hate me forever. I promise you that I'm gonna change and be a better person. Even if you never forgive me or stop hating me, please keep the money. I'll send more when I can.

Marcus

Coco wiped away her tears.

I've got to go see him. I'm still angry with Marcus, but I don't hate him. I need to tell him that.

Ransom was right, she decided. She should look deep within and not just at the outside. She closed her eyes and said a prayer for Marcus.

CHAPTER 17

"Knock knock."

Ransom looked up from his computer. "Kaitlin, come in."

He was glad to see his sister, but had hoped that it would be Coco standing at his door.

"How are you doing?" she asked him.

He got out of his chair and helped her into one. Ransom sat back down. "How are you and the little one?"

"We're doing great," she said. "Absolutely wonderful. I'm hoping he or she will decide to come before Christmas. Laine and Regis already have a Christmas baby. Jonathan was born on Christmas. Always complains that he's not getting his fair share of birthday and Christmas presents."

"I know that I haven't known you long, but I feel that you didn't just stop by to say hello."

"You're right. I didn't," she responded.

"Matt told me what happened. Are you and Coco okay?"

"Anything but," he said. "Things got real ugly between us the night Michael was shot. We haven't talked since then."

"So what are you waiting on, Ransom?"

"Kaitlin, I love Coco, but I don't think we have a future together."

"You don't if you don't talk to her and get this straightened out, that's for sure."

"That's just it. We can't resolve this, Kaitlin."

"You haven't tried," she countered. "Love is worth fighting for, Ransom. I can see the pain you're in. I know that you love Coco and that she loves you just as much. How can you walk away?"

"Kaitlin, that's not what I want. I love her and I thought we were trying to build a life together. But apparently I missed something."

"Then live up to your name," she stated. "Go after your woman. We Ransoms do not give up without a fight."

She started to rise to her feet. "I need to get going. My job here is done."

Ransom stood and walked over to his sister, helping her out of the chair. "Thanks for the pep talk."

"I'm glad I could dispense a little sisterly advice."

"Thank you for allowing me in your life, Kaitlin."

She hugged him. "We're family. I wouldn't have it any other way. Now don't forget what I've said, Ransom. You never give up on true love."

Kaitlin ordered a half-pound bag of raspberry chocolates, then said, "I just came from over at D-Unit, where I was seeing Ransom. Coco, I have to tell you — he looks about as sad as you do."

"I suppose he told you that we had a fight," she sighed. "Actually, I did all the fighting. I don't think I let him get in two words the entire time."

Kaitlin sat down at the counter. "All couples have disagreements."

Coco glanced up at her. "This was a big one, Kaitlin. I'm not sure we're going to be able to get past it."

"You will," Kaitlin said. "And I'll tell you why. Coco, you and Ransom love each other. I've seen the way the two of you look at one another. He's your soul mate, and trust me, everything will work out."

Coco didn't respond.

"He really loves you."

"I know," she said after a moment. "Kaitlin, I love him, too. But after what happened to my brother . . . I can't deal with those boys. Ransom has a lot of faith in them, while I don't trust them. How can we find a compromise in a situation like this?"

"Not all of them are bad, Coco."

"I hear what you're saying, Kaitlin. The boy involved in the robbery actually wrote me a letter apologizing, and he sent me ten dollars. But I need some time to recover from the shock of what happened."

Kaitlin nodded in understanding.

"How are things going with all of you?" Coco asked, changing the subject. "Has everyone adjusted to having Ransom as a brother?"

"I think so. We know that he's one of us. I just wish we could have grown up with him."

"How's the baby?"

Kaitlin smiled. "So far, the pregnancy is progressing naturally and the baby's healthy."

"I guess you guys decided to wait and be surprised?"

"Knowing would've made decorating easier. I know that Matt really wants a boy, so I figured it would be better to just wait and find out, in the event we're having another girl." Kaitlin eyed her. "What's wrong, Coco?"

"I miss him so much," she said. "I always felt like Ransom and I really fit, you know?"

"It's not over for you and him."

"I said some horrible things, Kaitlin. How can I ever expect him to forgive me? I really hurt him."

"We all hurt the ones we love at one time or another. Coco, it won't get any better if you two don't talk to each other. You have to communicate."

"I'm not sure I know what to say."

"Just wing it," Kaitlin suggested with a smile. "I have to go, but I want to hear something good soon."

When she left, Coco stared at the phone. "I can't do this," she whispered.

Coco sat in the visitors room at the L.A. County Jail. She'd never wanted to see the inside of a place like this. Never thought that she would.

This was only the visitors room. She couldn't imagine going into the bowels of the jailhouse.

Marcus, wearing blue scrubs like doctors wore, was escorted in by a guard.

He looks scared, she thought to herself. Really scared, and it broke her heart to see him that way.

"Miss Stanley, I didn't think you'd come."

"I almost didn't," she responded. "But not for the reasons you think. Marcus, I don't hate you, but I do feel betrayed by you. I never in a million years thought that you would do something like this. I really didn't. . . ."

He nodded. "I'm real sorry. I was at home talking about how fine you were and how nice you'd been to me. Miss Stanley, I had no idea that they were gonna rob you until that night."

"What about the other people in the neighborhood? Did you consider their feelings?"

"I didn't have nothing to do with them. That was all my brother and his friends."

Coco eyed him. "So you're telling me that you only participated in the one at my shop, then?"

"I already told Mr. Winters and the police all this. When I found out what was about to go down, I didn't want nobody to get hurt. I pleaded with my brother to take me along. I thought if I came, you'd be safe. I had nothing to do with the other robberies."

"I want to believe you."

"Miss Stanley, I'm not stupid. I knew you may recognize my custom-made shoes with my first name written all over them. If I wasn't trying to be caught, do you think I'd wear them to a robbery? I was hoping that Mr. Winters would be there with you."

"But you ran away before the cops came."

He shook his head. "I flagged them down and told them what happened. I turned myself in. You can ask them."

"That's why you called out to me in the shop," Coco said. "You were hoping I would catch on to your voice."

"I don't know what it would've accomplished. All I know is that I don't want to be anywhere near my brother. He's crazy. He beats on my mother and she's scared of him. I'm scared of him."

"Is he here?"

Marcus nodded. "He's threatening to kill me."

Coco could see how really scared he was — this was no act. "Have you told Ransom?"

"He's hired a lawyer for me and they are trying to work out some kind of deal. I testify against my brother and his friends and they are going to try and find someplace safe for me. Mr. Winters is looking into a boarding school somewhere."

"He has a lot of faith in you, Marcus."

"What about you?"

"The betrayal stings, but one day it will disappear. You accepted your part in this, even though you say that you were trying to protect us. From the sounds of it, you tried to find a way to put an end to the robberies. You took a stand and I can appreciate that, Marcus. I don't hate you and I do forgive you."

Tears rolled down his cheeks. "I never wanted to disappoint you or Mr. Winters."

"You should never want to disappoint yourself," Coco told him. "Marcus, I'm going to be okay after a while. Are you? Can you forgive yourself?"

He shrugged.

"Marcus, look at me."

He met her gaze.

"I'm proud of you for trying to set things right. That takes a lot of courage. When I look at you, I don't see the boy that you are now, but I see the man that you can become."

Their time was up.

"Thank you for coming, Miss Stanley."

"Marcus, you don't owe me anything, so I put the ten dollars on your account so that you're able to purchase whatever you might need in here. I also brought you a Bible, some magazines and snacks. What you can do for me is look deep within and find the man that Ransom and I see. Become this man and that is payment enough."

"Yes, ma'am."

"Take care of yourself."

"Please keep me in your prayers."

"I will," Coco promised.

On the way home, she called Ransom, but reached his voice mail. She left him a message.

"Ransom, it's me again," she said, a couple of hours later. "I'm calling to apologize for overreacting. I didn't exactly want to do it via voice mail, but you've left me no choice. I'm very sorry for the way I carried on. I know that not all of your students are criminals. Deep down, I really know that, but when my brother was shot — it scared me."

She paused for a moment before continuing. "I hope that you'll call me back so that we can talk. Ransom, I really miss you and I know that we can work this out. I'm truly sorry."

Coco hung up.

"Have you talked to Ransom?" Michael asked when he phoned her that evening.

"He's not returning my calls," she replied.

"You know what? I think he's out of town."

"How do you know that?" Coco asked.

"He never said anything to me."

"You weren't exactly talking to him, sis. Ransom called to check on me a couple of days ago, and he mentioned that he had to go out of town on business."

"He's still getting his messages, I'm sure."

"Coco, give him some time. Ransom will phone you when he's ready to talk to you. You both probably needed a cooling period."

She wasn't so sure.

She had really messed up this time. Coco had learned something about herself through all this — that she was quick to judge. She had never pictured herself in this light and she was ashamed.

This was not the type of person she wanted to be.

It was time to make some changes in her own life before she tried to work on somebody else's.

Ransom picked up the phone to call Coco, and then suddenly changed his mind. He was not going to give up on his students. She had no idea what Marcus had done to try and put his brother behind bars, at the risk of his own freedom.

A couple of his former students ended up in trouble again. One was recently caught trying to break into a home. There were those who slipped through the cracks from time to time, but it was a risk he was willing to take.

However, he wasn't willing to risk the lives of those he cared about. Over the past few days, he'd spent a lot of time trying to figure out a better way to screen students before allowing them entry into the program.

He believed he had come up with a plan, but wanted to run it by Ray and Matt first.

Ransom missed Coco. He missed her laughter — everything about her. Nothing felt right since that night.

He was surprised when he saw that she'd called. Even more when she actually left a message on his voice mail — an apology.

Ransom understood totally why she was so upset, but he wasn't just going to pull the plug on the program — there were too many success stories. They far outweighed the one incident.

The program worked.

Hopefully, Coco would one day see that for herself. He couldn't give up on those boys. They deserved a chance in this world and Ransom intended to give it to them.

He eyed the phone. "I miss you, Coco."

Then call her, his heart whispered.

He picked up the telephone and dialed.

"Hello . . ."

His heart skipped a beat at the sound of her voice. "It's me," Ransom said. "I'm sorry for just getting back to you, but I was out of town on business."

"My brother mentioned that you were away," Coco said. "Did you enjoy your trip?"

"It was okay," he answered. "To tell the truth, I missed you."

"Ransom, I missed you, too. At first I thought you were just ignoring me. I didn't know that you were on a business trip."

"It wasn't all business. I took a couple of days to try and figure out what my next steps should be," he admitted. "I'm really sorry about what happened to Michael. It was unfortunate. But I'm glad that the persons responsible are behind bars. It's the third strike for Marcus's brother, so he'll be doing the max."

"That's good to hear. Ransom, I was wrong when I said it was your fault. I never should've said something so mean to you."

"Coco, I don't really want to have this conversation over the phone. I'm dead tired, so I'm going to bed early, but if you're not busy tomorrow after church, can we get together and talk then? Are you going to your parents' for dinner?"

"No, I'll wait here for you," she responded. "Ransom, I'm glad you called."

He smiled. "True love never gives up."

CHAPTER 18

Ransom wasn't sure what he was going to say to Coco, but he knew that it was time for them to have a serious talk about their relationship.

He pulled into the driveway and parked the car.

Coco opened the front door just as he walked up to the porch.

"Hey," she murmured in greeting.

He embraced her, holding her tight. Ransom inhaled deeply, sucking in the light floral scent of her perfume. "I've missed you so much."

They stepped away from each other.

"It's time we made some decisions about our relationship and where we're going with it," he blurted. "That's why I'm here."

Coco nodded. "I thought as much."

They sat down in the living room.

"I love you with my whole heart, but I have to know that we are on the same page when it comes to D-Unit."

Her head snapped up. "I went to see Marcus at the jail. He told me everything. I've made a horrible rush to judgment, Ransom — I can't deny that. I just want you to know that I'm truly sorry for everything I said to you the night Michael was shot. I hope that one day you'll find it in your heart to forgive me." Coco paused for a moment, before continuing. "I love you so much, Ransom, and I want to be with you."

"I love you, too, Coco. Sweetheart, I never stopped loving you. I just don't know if we can ever get past what happened. I honestly don't know . . ."

She sighed in resignation. "Ransom, I know how much those boys mean to you. I know the heart you have for the youth. I won't try to stand in your way. I will support you fully on this."

"Honey, I know that you believe this, but what if something else happens? What then? I don't want to put you or anyone else at risk."

Coco began to cry. "I'm sorry. I said I wasn't going to do this."

He hugged her. "I hate to see you so sad. I don't want to hurt you, Coco."

She placed a finger to his lips. "I did this, Ransom. All of this is my fault."

Ransom surprised himself when he kissed her.

Coco responded by kissing him back passionately.

Desire ignited in the pit of his belly, the flames growing. He had to fight the urge to take Coco upstairs and make love to her.

She must have sensed his withdrawal, because she moved away from him. "Ransom, I want to be with you. I'm willing to take the risk if you are. Marcus isn't a bad kid. I realized that when I read his letter. I came to that conclusion before I even went to see him. It's why I went to the jail."

"I know that not every boy will be saved, but Coco, I can't give up on them."

"I do understand that," she told him. "Ransom, I applaud your dedication. The ones that I've met so far really have a desire to change, and they deserve a chance. But there are those that don't want to do anything to better their lives."

"I met with my staff and we've decided to implement a thorough screening process that includes notification of gang affiliations, criminal records, etc. Ray and I have talked, and he's going to help me set everything up. I have a meeting with a friend of his, A. C. Richards, on Tuesday. I hear she's looking to help teens stay out of gangs. She worked with Matt and is a very good detective, from what I hear. I'm hoping she'll be willing to come on board."

"She helped Matt get Kaitlin out of Mexico," Coco told him. "She and her sister own a detective agency called Richardson & Associates."

"I think I've heard of them. That's good." He paused. "I'm not going to lie to you. It's going to get rough sometimes, Coco. Are you sure you want this in your life?"

"I want you, Ransom, and everything that comes with you. We haven't lost our love for each other — the kiss proved that. I know I've said it before, but I truly mean it this time."

"I believe you," he said, smiling.

Coco met his gaze. "Ransom, I can't see my life without you in it. These past two weeks have been so miserable. I definitely wasn't looking forward to Christmas."

He broke into a smile. "To be honest, I wasn't, either. I'm glad you called, because I was going to return all of your gifts tomorrow."

She stepped away from him. "Are you serious?"

He nodded. "You didn't think I was still going to give them to you, did you?"

"I've been good all year," she said. "Well,

most of it, anyway."

"You'd have to take that up with Santa."

"I don't believe in Santa."

Ransom laughed. "You're gorgeous when you pout."

"But you've changed your mind, right?"

"I'm considering it."

"What do you mean by that?" Coco asked, her arms folded across her chest.

"I'm kidding," Ransom responded with a chuckle. "So what do we do now, Coco?" he asked.

"Get our relationship back on track," she said. "We can start by you helping me prepare dinner. Then we can go to the mall and pick out some gifts for Cinna."

He smiled. "Sounds like a plan to me."

Pulling her closer to him, Ransom covered her lips with his, kissing her hungrily. "I'm so glad to have you back, sweetheart," he whispered.

She loved Ransom more than life itself and never tired of looking at him.

Standing by him in the kitchen, Coco openly admired Ransom as he prepared a roast to put in the oven. The man was fine, loving, had a generous heart and could cook like nobody's business.

"You finished with the potatoes?" he asked.

"Almost," she responded. Coco had forgotten what she was doing, caught up in eying Ransom.

"You got the invitation to the Christmas party?" Ransom asked.

"The one from Laine? Yeah. I wasn't going to go, but now that we're getting back on track, I think we should go together."

He agreed.

"That's this coming Friday, right?"

"Yeah," he replied.

She handed him the bowl of potatoes.

"Thanks, sweetheart," he murmured, concentrating on the food.

It feels good to have him back in my life.

Coco smiled at the thought.

Ransom stuck the roast into the preheated oven.

Then he reached out and embraced her, the warmth of his arms radiating through her. Her lips turned upward even more as she leaned back against him.

The telephone rang.

It was Elle.

"Kaitlin's at the hospital," she told Coco. "She's in labor."

"Elle, Ransom's here with me. We'll be right there."

"Don't forget your camera."

"I won't," Coco declared.

She hung up. "So much for dinner. We'll have to grab something on the way to the hospital."

They turned everything off, then rushed out of the house.

"I never knew that having a baby could be a family event," Ransom stated. "I always thought of it as private — between the couple."

"This is your family's tradition," Coco teased. "I'm all for the private birth event."

Twenty minutes later, the two of them walked down the hallway to the maternity center.

Jillian was standing outside the room when they arrived.

"How is she?" Coco asked.

"She's doing fine. Just begged the doctor for some drugs." Jillian chuckled. "I told her she was going to need them, but she wanted to experience natural childbirth first."

They heard the shrill screaming of a young woman in the room next door.

"Oh, my goodness," Coco muttered. "The poor girl."

They were at the hospital exactly one hour before Chandler St. Charles made his entrance into the world.

Matt was ecstatic and Kaitlin was relieved that the whole ordeal was over.

She smiled when she saw Coco and Ransom walk into the room together. "I'm glad you both listened to me."

Coco held up the camera. "Let me know when you're ready for pictures."

Kaitlin raised a hand. "Give me a minute." She glanced over at Elle and said, "Could you do something with this hair on my head? Throw a little powder on my face and I'll be ready to go."

Coco couldn't help feeling a little envious. Kaitlin, Elle, all of them except Ivy had the type of marriages people read about. She wanted that for herself. Coco found that she was yearning to be a mother, too.

She was ready, but what about Ransom? It was much too soon to bring up the subject now. They had just gotten back together.

Coco decided to just take one day at a time. If she and Ransom were meant to be, she wanted it to happen naturally, without any pressure.

The holidays were over and a New Year begun. It was time for Coco to start preparing for her biggest month of the year —

February. Valentine's Day was less than a month away.

Ransom had been spending a lot of time with his partner, writing songs for a debut artist. Between his hours at the center and with Jaye, he and Coco hadn't been able to spend quality time together.

She didn't complain, though. She had been busy with Michael and Daniel, brainstorming new product ideas. She had come up with new items for valentines and for her sensual line.

The door to the shop opened.

It was Jerome.

"Hey you," she said in greeting. "Did you have a good time during your Christmas break? Ransom told me that you went to Florida to see your grandparents."

"It was nice. We had a good time." He walked over to the broom closet. "I'ma sweep up this place for you. You need to tell your customers to stop tracking in dirt. This is a high-class place and they need to treat it like one."

Valencia and Coco exchanged amused glances.

"What's going on, Jerome?" Coco asked. She had gotten to know him well enough to know that there was something bothering him. "Come talk to me. You can sweep later if you want, but you don't have to — I can do it after we close."

"Miss Stanley, I can't find no job. I even asked your brother, but he don't have any openings right now."

"Has something happened?" she inquired.

"My mom lost her job. We might have to move to Florida unless she can find something else here. She was down there looking for a job."

"Florida is a nice place to live."

"If you like hurricanes," he muttered in response.

"What is the real reason you don't want to go to Florida?" Coco asked.

"I don't want to leave you and Mr. Winters. You two keep me straight."

She shook her head. "No, *you* keep you straight, Jerome. You purposed in your heart that you would become a better you. Ransom and I can't take credit for that."

"It might be good," Jerome said after a moment. "I can get away from these knuckleheads."

"Didn't you tell me at one time that you wanted to go to college in Florida?"

He nodded.

"Well, Florida can't be too bad, then."

"I'd miss you and Mr. Winters."

"There's e-mail," she said with a chuckle.

"And you love texting. He and I both have unlimited texting."

"I know that you were real hurt when Marcus and his brother came here. Marcus an all right dude. He just got a crazy brother."

"I'm glad Ransom was able to get him away from here," she said. "His brother is going to prison for a long time."

"Miss Stanley, thank you for seeing me as a person and for not thinking that we're all thugs. I'm not the clothes I wear."

"No, you're not," she said. "Most times, people don't take time to look past the clothing. You, Benjamin and even Marcus have taught me to look past the outer shell to the inner man. Thank you for that gift, Jerome."

"You're not gonna start crying now, are you?" he asked with a frown.

Coco laughed as a tear ran down her cheek.

CHAPTER 19

It was Sunday.

Ransom, his brothers and Michael were in Miami for the Super Bowl.

Coco surfed through the channels on her television, searching for something to watch, but there wasn't a whole lot to choose from. She had a slight temperature and felt weak from a spell of the flu. She'd had enough of Lifetime movies and wasn't interested in watching the pregame events.

Her mother walked into the room. "How are you feeling, sugar?" She sat down on the chair across from her.

Coco could feel her mom's eyes on her and met her gaze. "I wish Ransom was here."

"They'll be back tomorrow."

"I know." She sighed.

"Are you hungry?"

Coco shook her head. She didn't believe she could keep anything down. She hated being sick.

"Mama, you don't have to stay here. I don't want *you* getting sick."

"I had my flu shot. I keep telling you to get one."

"Maybe next year," Coco said. She leaned back against the sofa, her eyes closed. Ransom had offered to come home when he found out she was sick, but Coco knew how much he had been looking forward to the game.

Her mother's words broke through her musings. "You're sure you don't want to try eating something?"

Coco shook her head again. "Not right now, Mama. Maybe in a little while."

February 1

Coco was feeling stronger, but decided to stay home for another day. Actually, Ransom insisted that she take one more day off before diving back into her work.

Michael assured her that Valencia had everything under control.

The knock on the door surprised Coco.

She opened it and smiled. "What are you doing here? I thought you were going to be at the studio all day long."

"I wanted to make sure you were behaving."

"I'm here," she said. "I'm bored to tears, though."

Ransom held up a bag. "I brought you some lunch. You need to eat so that you can gain back some of the weight you lost."

Coco frowned. "I hope that's not soup."

"It's not."

"Good. Because I'm really sick of soup."

"It's from La Maison. Matt told me that you love the red beans and rice."

"Yes!" she squealed.

Ransom laughed.

They sat down at the table and talked while she ate her lunch. When she was done, they went into the den.

"I have something else for you," Ransom announced with a smile.

Her eyes grew hopeful. "Dessert?"

He shook his head.

She tried to hide her disappointment.

Ransom handed her a box.

"What's this for?" she asked.

"The first day of February," Ransom said. "And the first of fourteen presents. I'm giving you one a day until Valentine's Day."

Excited, Coco unwrapped her gift. She laughed when she saw the gleaming set of ebony chopsticks. "This is from our first date. When you tried to teach me to eat with them. I ruined that beautiful silk shirt of yours."

"I was enjoying your company so much that I barely noticed," he said. "It was one of the best nights of my life."

She kissed him. "Mine, too."

Coco had already purchased a gift for him — tickets to join his siblings on their annual family cruise. This year they were sailing the Mediterranean. She was joining him, although they were going to have separate cabins.

She had learned a long time ago never to ponder what she was getting for Valentine's Day. That way she didn't have to deal with disappointment. However, it was hard to escape the excitement and anticipation of daily presents until "V" day. Coco was touched by his creativity.

The next day, when he picked her up for dinner, Ransom gave Coco another gift.

Without saying a word, she tore into the package. "It's a CD of the concert we went to," she exclaimed. "That was our second or third date. I love it."

She leaned over and kissed him on the cheek.

"I'm glad you like the gifts."

"I'm warning you, Ransom, you're spoiling me with all these presents. A girl could get used to this very quickly. I love receiving gifts."

"Good," he responded. "I love giving them to you."

He was looking forward to Valentine's Day, because that was when he would give her the most important gift — the gift of his heart and soul.

CHAPTER 20

Ransom serenaded Coco with a song he'd written for her, and feeling ambitious, actually attempted to play it on the violin.

" 'I've often heard that for every heart, there beats another, a matter of time until someday you find each other. But Coco, each night when I look up to the skies, I wonder out of all the millions, will the real one pass me by?

" 'But now I believe in all the joy and laughter I see in your gorgeous eyes. I know we'll endure forever and a day. Every dream that I dream can come true, 'cause out of all the millions, Coco, I found you . . .' "

Ransom cleared his throat, then sang, " 'Baby, I don't wanna miss this chance to say that nobody ever touched me in the way that you have. Every dream that I have, I know can come true, 'cause I found you. Yeah o' yeah . . . I found you.' "

The words were beautiful but his attempts

to play the violin were disastrous.

Coco put a hand to her mouth to keep from chuckling. She didn't want to hurt his feelings after he had worked so hard to try and play the violin. It was terribly romantic, but poor Ransom — he wasn't a bad singer, but playing the violin was not his gift.

She clapped as loud and as hard as she could when he was done.

"Baby, that was one of the most romantic gestures anyone has ever done for me. Thank you," she told him. "I loved every minute of it."

"I recorded it on a CD for you and it sounds much better than the live version. Play it when you are in need of a laugh every now and then."

"Ransom, I love it because I know that it came from your heart," she stated, holding the CD to her own heart. "I'm going to cherish this forever."

"There are a couple of other songs on the CD," Ransom said. "They are a blend of hip-hop and violin music. I think it came out really nice."

"Really?" Coco rose to her feet. "I'd like to hear it."

She walked over to the CD player and slipped in the disk, then stood there listening, amazed at the results. "This is nice, baby."

Inspired, she and Ransom spent the rest of the evening putting music to the song he'd written for her.

"I like that," he said at last.

"You can even add some rap to it for the remix. Like this." Coco stood up. "You say you love . . . yeah . . . yeah. You make my heart sing. . . ."

"Honey, just stick to playing the violin," Ransom advised, laughing hard.

She threw a pillow at him.

CHAPTER 21

Valentine's Day

Ransom had given her chopsticks, CDs, a song he'd written just for her, a huge box of red hots candy, a pair of heart-printed socks, personalized cards, plus handwritten love notes that she'd found planted in her coat pocket, in the refrigerator and behind the windshield wiper of her car. He had sent her flowers, fourteen perfect red roses. A hilarious Valentine's Day T-shirt. A bag of candy hearts personalized with their names. A beautiful teddy bear, and a host of other cute romantic gifts.

Coco stared at the stunning red gown, Ransom's most recent present to her, along with a formal invitation to meet him at La Maison for a very special Valentine's Day dinner. She fingered the expensive material of the dress. This was by far the most extravagant of the gifts, although she knew the studio time for the CDs must have set him back a few hundred dollars.

No man had ever done anything like this for her. Coco knew she shouldn't be surprised — look at the way he was with his boys. Ransom was generous to a fault.

Smiling, she padded barefoot to the shower. She was not going to be late for her romantic evening with Ransom.

She showered quickly, then got out and dried off. Coco ran her fingers through her short curly hair. She eyed her reflection, scrutinizing her complexion, then applied her makeup with a light hand.

Satisfied with her looks, she got up and slipped on the strapless gown. It fit her body as if it had been made just for her.

"Great job, Ransom," she whispered. She was pretty sure his sisters must have helped choose her gown. Kaitlin owned a chain of bridal stores, so she was probably the one who'd selected this gift.

Coco would be arriving at La Maison any moment now. The driver had called to let him know that they were a block away. Ransom and Matt had worked on the perfect menu for this evening — everything had to be perfect.

Coco took his breath away when she walked into the private dining room at La

Maison restaurant wearing the stunning red strapless gown he'd purchased for her.

She glanced around the room. "Are more people joining us?"

"Yes, but before they get here, I want to do this."

He kissed her.

"Hey, get a room."

They turned around to find Kaitlin standing in the doorway.

"You look stunning," she told Coco. "Have you seen my husband?"

"Are you joining us for dinner?"

Kaitlin nodded.

Just then Ray and Carrie arrived, followed by more of the Ransom clan.

"You don't mind that dinner is more of a family affair, do you?" Ransom asked.

"Of course not," Coco responded. She spied Michael walking in with Ivy, and waved. "You invited my parents, too?"

Ransom nodded. "We're going to celebrate Valentine's Day as a family."

"This is really nice," she told him.

"Elle, what's wrong?" Coco asked a moment later, noting the troubled expression on her friend's face. "Has something happened?"

"Mama's bringing a date."

"Really?"

"I mean, she deserves to have a life, but none of us knew she was dating anyone."

"Maybe he's just a companion or a good friend," Coco offered.

"Maybe," Elle responded. "I just need to wrap my head around her seeing someone."

When everyone had arrived, Matt came in and greeted them.

"Tonight, we will dine on oysters Rockefeller, chateaubriand with portobello mushrooms and Madeira wine jus, steamed asparagus with hollandaise sauce, twice-baked potatoes with leeks and parmesan. For dessert, we will have tiramisu hearts, and we would be remiss if we didn't end the evening with coffee and Stanley white-chocolate dipped strawberries."

Waiters appeared out of nowhere, bringing in trays of food as soft jazz floated around the room.

Ransom reached over and took Coco's hand in his.

"Did you plan all this?" she asked him.

"Matt helped."

"You did all this for us?"

He nodded. "My mom and I used to do Valentine's Day in a big way. We'd get all dressed up and go to dinner."

"This is very nice. If she's looking down here right now, I'm sure she's happy and smiling."

"I think so, too. This is what she wanted for me." Ransom glanced around the room.

"I think they're all in shock, seeing Miss Amanda with another man."

"She's never shown any interest in dating before. I'm surprised myself, but that does explain why she's doing all these spa days with my mom. Aunt Amanda never really cared about stuff like that before."

Laine said grace.

Everyone dived into their food.

After dinner, it was time for the couples to exchange gifts.

Ransom was speechless when Coco gave him trip cruise tickets. "We go on a cruise every year," Kaitlin explained. "Since you're one of us, we are expecting you to join us this year."

"Coco, I can't believe that you did this for me," he told her. "A cruise to the Mediterranean."

"You're going to be with your family — and me, of course. I hope you don't mind that I decided to tag along."

"I wouldn't have it any other way," Ransom said with a smile. "I noticed you reserved two cabins."

She lowered her voice to a whisper. "I know that you're celibate and I didn't want to tempt you too much by being in the same room with you."

He laughed. "Coco, I think that it's time for me to give you my gift."

Ransom pulled a present from under the table.

Coco hid her disappointment.

Well, that's certainly too big to be jewelry. It's not like I was expecting a ring or anything, but couldn't the man have bought me earrings or a bracelet?

Shut up! I'm happy with whatever Ransom gives me.

Smiling, Coco unwrapped the package. Inside was an elegant wooden box, which she opened to find a large diamond-shaped chocolate candy inside, inscribed with the words *Will you marry me?*

Coco blinked twice, then read it again. " 'Will you marry me?' " She met Ransom's emotion-filled gaze. "Is this for real?"

He nodded. "I love you, Constance Stanley, and I want you to be my wife."

She kissed him. "I love you, too, and yes, I'll marry you."

Ransom grinned. "We're not done yet. Now for the other part of your gift." He pulled a tiny black velvet box out of his pocket.

He opened it to reveal a gorgeous diamond engagement ring featuring a four-carat, emerald-cut, chocolate diamond with two white diamonds along the shank. "The diamonds are all conflict-free, something we both feel strongly about."

Tears rolled down Coco's cheeks. "It's stunning," she whispered.

The room erupted in applause.

Coco pulled him to her and kissed him. "Thank you for the honor of being your fiancée. Now tell me, what kind of candy is this?"

Ransom smiled. "This diamond has a Venezuelan chocolate casing with a rich praline center."

Coco glanced over her shoulder at her brother. "Michael told you this was my favorite, right?"

"It isn't?"

"No, it's just that I always told him that the man I married would bring me pralines covered in Venezuelan chocolate."

Ransom gave Michael a thumbs-up. "Good looking out, man."

"Hey, it's the ultimate chocolate proposal," he responded.

Coco was all smiles for the rest of the evening. This was a Valentine's Day she would never forget.

CHAPTER 22

Holy Trinity Christian Church was filled to capacity.

This was the first wedding to be performed in the new building. The chic architectural lines of the structure provided the perfect backdrop for Ransom and Coco's June wedding. The rows of seats were garnished with lavish displays of red and ivory flowers arranged with bronze-colored ribbons and baby's breath.

Coco stood in front of a huge full-length mirror in the bridal dressing room. She had never been to a church with a room set aside specifically for brides and their attendants.

This is pretty cool.

"You look so beautiful," Elle said from behind her. "I can't wait to glimpse Ransom's face when he sees you walking down the aisle."

"So do you," she responded, turning

around to face her best friend. "That mocha color looks great on you."

Coco had chosen to have her bridesmaids wear different shades of chocolate, from deep dark chocolate to a creamy mocha color. Her own gown was the color of white chocolate.

The men were all wearing dark brown, custom-designed tuxedos, their vests in varying shades to match the bridesmaid dresses.

Coco had been fortunate to find a flower grower that had chocolate-colored blooms available. Chocolate orchids, chocolate cosmos and chocolate sundae dahlias were used in her wedding bouquet and the decorations for the reception.

Her father came to the door. "It's time," he said with a smile.

Elle hugged her. "I'll see you at the altar."

"Baby, I'm so happy for you," Coco's dad murmured. "You got yourself a good man. If Prescott were here, I know that he'd be pleased."

"Thank you, Daddy, for setting a perfect example of a good man," Coco told him. "You were my first date and you set the standard by which I chose the men in my life. I love you."

"I love you and I'm so very proud of you."

He gestured toward the door. "Now let's not keep your husband-to-be waiting."

She grinned. "That has such a nice ring to it."

Moments later, Coco floated down the aisle on her father's arm toward the man she would love forever.

They stood facing each other as they said their vows.

Coco spoke first. "Ransom, you are my one true love and I take you to be my husband. I will cherish our union and love you more each day than I did the day before. I will trust you and respect you, laugh with you and cry with you, loving you faithfully through good times and bad, regardless of the obstacles we may face together. I give you my hand, my heart and my love, from this day forward for as long as we both shall live."

"Constance, I love you. You are my best friend and today I give myself to you in marriage. I want you to know that I eagerly anticipate the chance to grow together, getting to know the woman you will become and falling in love a little more every day. I promise to encourage and inspire you, to laugh with you, and to comfort you in times of sorrow and struggle. I promise to love and cherish you through whatever life may bring us. These things I give to you today, and all the days of our life."

Coco could hardly contain her excitement as she waited to hear the words that would make their union real to her.

"I now pronounce you man and wife . . ."

Ransom exhaled a long sigh of pleasure. He felt as if he had been waiting a very long time to hear those words, but in reality it had been only four months. Neither one of them wanted a long engagement.

He pulled Coco into his arms, drawing her close. He pressed his lips to hers for a chaste, yet meaningful kiss.

Grinning, Ransom escorted his bride down the aisle and through the double exit doors at the back of the church. They escaped into a nearby room, waiting until it was time to go back into the chapel for the wedding photographs.

His eyes traveled down the length of her, nodding in obvious approval. "You look so beautiful, sweetheart."

Coco broke into a big smile. "We're married." She held up her left hand to show off the wedding set. "I can truly say that this is the happiest day of my life."

After the photographs, they were driven to La Maison for the reception.

In continuing with the chocolate theme, there were several chocolate fountains throughout the room surrounded by bowls of fresh fruit.

Their wedding menu consisted of duck with chocolate sauce, chocolate-dusted scallops with vanilla butter sauce, chicken mole, and seared pork tenderloin with cocoa spice rub. Guests had a choice of two of the four entrées, mixed vegetables, yellow rice and an assortment of rolls.

On each table were stacks of elegantly designed boxes of chocolate truffles in a variety of flavors that had been created just for their wedding.

"Do you think we got a little carried away with the chocolate theme?" Ransom asked in a low voice.

Coco looked up at him. "Honey, chocolate has always been associated with love. What better way to celebrate one of the most memorable days of our lives than with chocolate? It's not just a girl's best friend. It's the food of love."

Ransom guided Coco over to their table and pulled out a chair for her.

They had preselected their meals, so their plates arrived shortly after they sat down.

Ransom dined on the duck with chocolate sauce and the scallops, while Coco enjoyed the chicken mole as her entrée.

Her eyes bounced around the room. "This is the same room where you asked me to marry you."

"This is where you made me the happiest man alive."

Coco smiled. "And here we are. We're married."

Ransom nodded. "We're starting a new life together."

After they finished eating, the bride and groom stood up and headed to the middle of the room to dance for the first time as husband and wife.

The song ended and another began while they were still on the dance floor. Ransom only had eyes for Coco. "I love you, sweetheart. With every fiber of my being, I love you."

"I love you back," she told him. "I still can't believe that we pulled this together in four months."

"I didn't want to go on that cruise with you and have to sleep in separate cabins." He bent his head and whispered in her ear, "I am ready to make you mine completely."

"I've been waiting for you to say those words for such a long time."

Jerome walked up and cleared his throat, letting them know that they were no longer alone. "Congratulations. I guess I have to get used to calling you Mrs. Winters now."

She hugged him. "I'm so glad you were able to come. How are things?"

"Great. I'm liking Florida a lot."

"See, I told you."

"I'm playing football next year for my high school. Can't believe that I'm going to be a sophomore. Coach said he thinks I'm good enough to maybe get an athletic scholarship for college. He was driving by and saw me playing with my cousins in the street. He says I have natural ability."

"Now look at that," Ransom said. "Tell your coach that you have something else. Heart."

The teen grinned. "Thanks for flying me in for the wedding."

"We wouldn't have had it any other way, Jerome. Enjoy the party."

Benjamin came up next. "Mr. and Mrs. W. Congrats. Y'all look good together and I hope you know that this is serious. You can't get mad and go running off. You stay and fight. Two very special people in my life told me that once."

Coco embraced him. "I will always remember this. Oh, I hear that your mother is off the chemo and doing well."

He nodded. "She's cancer free. I give

thanks to the Lord for that. And one more thing. I got accepted into California State University Long Beach. The letter came right before I left for the wedding. It's out in the car."

"That's great," Ransom said, looking like a proud parent. "Congratulations. I'll be on my honeymoon for two weeks, but as soon as I get back, we'll sit down and take care of tuition."

"Benjamin's tuition is going to be covered by me."

They turned to find Coco's father standing there. "He's a Stanley employee and we have a scholarship with his name on it. You have great potential and we're all proud of you, son."

Benjamin hugged the newlyweds and then walked off with his benefactor.

"Your boys are becoming men," Coco told Ransom.

He nodded. "Yes, they are."

"Now you're really my sister," Elle said when she walked up to them. "I'm so happy for you both."

Ransom placed his arms around his bride. "I love this woman more than my own life. I never really understood what that meant until now."

Brennan joined them. "I feel the same way

about Elle. She's the better part of me."

"All this love in the air is sickening," Ivy murmured as she brushed past them. She met Michael and they made their way out of the hotel ballroom.

"Ivy and your brother sure have been spending a lot of time together," Elle said. "What do you think is going on there?"

Coco shrugged. "I don't know, but you're right, Elle. They were together on Valentine's Day, then last night at the rehearsal dinner, and now they seem inseparable."

When the two of them returned, Ivy was laughing at something Michael was saying.

"Hmm . . ." Coco studied her brother's face. "He's really animated. Look at him."

"They look good together," Elle said.

Ransom grabbed Coco by the hand. "C'mon. Let's just enjoy our day. No match-making."

Brennan laughed. "That includes you, too, sweetie."

"Well, they would make a great couple," Coco said as they walked back to their table. "Michael needs somebody like Ivy in his life. All he does is work."

Ransom kissed his bride to quiet her.

"I know what you're trying to do," she told him. "But it's not going to work. My brother is a good man, and besides, they used to date and —"

He kissed her again.

"You are really trying to shut me up."

"No," Ransom responded. "I just love kissing you."

Coco grinned. "Okay, I like that answer, so I'll leave it at that."

He laughed, then asked, "Are you ready to leave?"

Her lips turned upward as she thought of what was to come. "Yeah. Let's get out of here. You go say goodbye to your family and I'll say goodbye to mine."

Ransom shook his head. "You're my wife now, sweetheart. We'll take time to say goodbye to our combined family together. We are all family now."

"You're right."

"Are you ready to make the first of our babies?"

Coco smiled and nodded.

"Auntie Coco, are you leaving now?"

She turned around to face her niece. "Yeah, sweetie. We're getting ready to leave."

"Can I give my new uncle a hug?"

Ransom nodded. "You sure can," he told her.

Cinnamon embraced him. "You smell so good," she exclaimed. "When I get married, I want the groom to wear that cologne. Can you save a bottle?"

Coco chuckled, while Ransom held back a smile. "I'll do what I can, cutie," he promised.

Giggling, Cinnamon looked up at her aunt. "Auntie, I'm gonna love him. He called me *cutie.*"

Coco hugged her. "We'll see you when we get back from our honeymoon, Cinna."

"Can I come over and stay with y'all for, like, two or three days when you get back?" she asked, her eyes full of hope.

"Of course you can, sweetie," Coco and Ransom declared in unison.

"She's so adorable," he said when Cinnamon ran off to find her mother. "Oh, and honey, I know how much you love chocolate, but we are not naming our children Mocha, Caramel or anything like that."

"Caramel is not a chocolate, but point taken," Coco told him. "We'll find meaningful names that don't include anything in the chocolate family."

"You're really okay with that?"

She nodded. "I think what you name your child should have special meaning to the parents."

They said their goodbyes and headed out of the room to a suite upstairs that had been reserved for them. Ransom and Coco would spend their wedding night there and then fly out the next morning to Antigua for the first leg of their honeymoon. From there, they would fly to Europe.

In the suite, Ransom unbuttoned the back of Coco's wedding gown.

"I'm going to have a bath."

"How about I join you?" he whispered.

She flashed him a sexy smile. "I was so hoping you'd say that."

He followed her into the bathroom.

After a long, sensual bath together, Ransom dried her off with a soft fluffy towel.

Coco gloried in their shared moment, wrapped in a silken cocoon of euphoria. If time stopped right this moment, she wouldn't complain. Life just couldn't get any better for her as far as she was concerned.

They slipped on matching terry robes.

Munching on grapes, Coco sat down on the edge of the king-size bed, while Ransom opened the bottle of nonalcoholic champagne Matt and Kaitlin had sent to their room.

Ransom prepared a plate of cheese, grapes and crackers, which he carried over to the bed. He sat down beside his wife. "I never thought I could be this happy."

Coco glanced up at her husband. "I feel

the same way. I never really thought I'd get married. I was fine with that, but I am glad to have you in my life."

"You make me so happy."

"Enough talking," she told him. "If we're serious about starting our own family, then we need to get busy."

Ransom grinned. His deepest desires had come true. He had a relationship with his siblings and he was married to the gorgeous woman in bed with him.

He sent up a quick prayer of thanksgiving before giving Coco his full attention.

ABOUT THE AUTHOR

Jacquelin Thomas is a bestselling author of more than thirty books and is an avid reader of romance novels when she's not writing. She and her family live in North Carolina, where she is busy working on her next book.

The employees of Thorndike Press hope you have enjoyed this Large Print book. All our Thorndike, Wheeler, and Kennebec Large Print titles are designed for easy reading, and all our books are made to last. Other Thorndike Press Large Print books are available at your library, through selected bookstores, or directly from us.

For information about titles, please call:
  (800) 223-1244

or visit our Web site at:
  http://gale.cengage.com/thorndike

To share your comments, please write:
  Publisher
  Thorndike Press
  295 Kennedy Memorial Drive
  Waterville, ME 04901